She shivered v [D0404482]

Along the bridge, the guardrails had collapsed and the structure appeared rickety. She peered at the water below as the cold seeped through her cape.

She'd been foolish to leave the security of Abram's home. But she needed to get to a computer.

Above the roar of the water she heard his voice.

"Miriam?"

Abram had come to stop her, yet he wasn't thinking of her own good—he was thinking of the other woman who'd worn this cape and *kapp*. His late wife.

"Go home, Abram."

Wind tore along the river, throwing her off balance, causing her to teeter toward the water. Her fall was aborted only by his strong hands.

"Let me go."

"No, Miriam. You must come with me."

"I won't. You can't control me."

"This time you must listen. He is coming for you."

Debby Giusti is an award-winning Christian author who met and married her military husband at Fort Knox, Kentucky. Together they traveled the world, raised three wonderful children and have now settled in Atlanta, Georgia, where Debby spins tales of mystery and suspense that touch the heart and soul. Visit Debby online at debbygiusti.com, blog with her at seekerville.blogspot.com and craftieladiesofromance.blogspot.com, and email her at Debby@DebbyGiusti.com.

Books by Debby Giusti

Love Inspired Suspense

Amish Protectors

Amish Refuge

Military Investigations

The Officer's Secret
The Captain's Mission
The Colonel's Daughter
The General's Secretary
The Soldier's Sister
The Agent's Secret Past
Stranded
Person of Interest
Plain Danger
Plain Truth

Visit the Author Profile page at Harlequin.com for more titles.

AMISH REFUGE

DEBBY GIUSTI

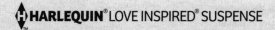
HARLEQUIN® LOVE INSPIRED® SUSPENSE

Recycling programs for this product may not exist in your area.

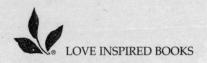

LOVE INSPIRED BOOKS

ISBN-13: 978-0-373-45705-2

Amish Refuge

Copyright © 2017 by Deborah W. Giusti

This edition published by arrangement with Love Inspired Books.

® and TM are trademarks of Love Inspired Books, used under license. Trademarks indicated with ® are registered in the United States Patent and Trademark Office, the Canadian Intellectual Property Office and in other countries.

www.Harlequin.com

Printed in U.S.A.

O Lord, You have been our refuge through all generations.
—*Psalms* 90:1

This story is dedicated
to my cousins—
David, Eric, Sandy and Bill—
for the wonderful memories
of going home to Ohio.

ONE

Serpent would find her and kill her. Tonight.

Miriam Miller woke with a start, chilled to the bone. She rubbed her hands over her arms and blinked against the night air seeping through the broken car window. Tugging her crocheted scarf and threadbare jacket across her chest, she straightened in the driver's seat and gazed through the windshield.

A police car with lights flashing braked to a stop on the edge of the narrow, two-lane road not more than twenty feet from where she'd parked, hidden by trees and underbrush.

Fear clutched her throat.

The cop—a bull of a man with a heart as dark as the night—stepped to the pavement and played his flashlight over the tall pines. Her pulse pounded and a roar filled her ears. She could envision the serpent tattoo that wrapped around his neck, the snake as heinous as the man.

She had been a fool to think she could elude him by hiding in the woods. Even more of a fool to succumb to the fatigue brought on by the drugs he had used to subdue her.

Fisting her hands, she swallowed the bile that filled her mouth and steeled her spine with resolve. He'd caught her once. He would never capture her again.

She reached for the key in the ignition and held her

breath as he pushed aside a tree branch and peered deeper into the woods. With the flick of his wrist, a flash of light caught her in its glare. Just that fast, he was running straight for her.

Before she could start the engine, he opened the driver's door and yanked her from the car. Screaming, she fell at his feet, crawled away on all fours and struggled to right herself.

He kicked her ribs. Air wheezed from her lungs. He grabbed her hair, turned her to face him and pulled her upright.

She thrashed her arms, kicked her feet then jabbed her fingers deep into his eyes.

He cursed, covered his face with his hands and stumbled backward. "Why you—!"

She lunged for her car.

A bag of craft supplies lay on the floor mat. Frantically she dug for the shears, relieved when her hand gripped the sharp steel.

He struck her shoulder, knocking her off balance. She cried in pain. Another blow, this one to her head.

She tightened her hold on the scissors, raised her hand and stabbed his neck. He groaned, momentarily stunned. She scrambled into her car, slammed and locked the door, and turned the key in the ignition. He grabbed the door handle and banged on the window, his hateful face pushed flat against the cracked glass.

The motor purred to life.

"Thank You," she silently prayed to a God in whom she'd only started to believe.

Serpent railed in rage.

She jammed the accelerator to the floorboard. Her head flew back as the sudden momentum jerked the car forward, throwing her attacker to the ground.

Her heart pounded nearly out of her chest and her hands shook so hard she could barely steer the car along the narrow path that led back to the pavement. She glanced at her rearview mirror.

Bathed in the red glow of her taillights, Serpent raised his fist, his curse faintly audible even over the hum of her engine.

Her stomach roiled.

She accelerated. The car fishtailed. Blood seeped from the gash to her forehead. She wiped her hand across her brow and blinked back the swell of panic that clamped down on her chest. Her breath caught as she glanced at her speedometer, knowing she was driving much too fast.

Her cell phone, with its dead battery, sat on the console. If she had a car charger, she would call for help. Not the authorities. She couldn't trust law enforcement, but her older sister, Hannah, would know what to do.

Headlights flashed in her rearview mirror. Her heart stopped. He was following her.

She increased her speed, all too aware of her threadbare tires and the threat of ice on the mountain road. The engine whined as she rounded a turn. Gripping the wheel, white-knuckled, she worked to hold the road.

Pop! The right rear tire deflated.

The blowout caused the car to shimmy across the pavement and career down a steep embankment. In the path of her headlights, she saw the river, edged with ice.

She screamed, anticipating the frigid water. Unable to swim, she'd drown. At the last second the car came to an abrupt halt, mired in mud. Her head hit the steering wheel. She moaned and blinked back the darkness that swirled around her.

A warning welled up from deep within her.

Run!

Dazed, she grabbed her phone, crawled from the car and

staggered into the woods. Pushing through brambles, she ignored the sharp thorns that scraped her arms and tugged at her jacket. A clearing lay ahead.

In the distance she saw a farmhouse. A warm glow beckoned from the downstairs window. She turned to see the police cruiser racing down the hill, seemingly oblivious to where her car had gone off the road.

Could Serpent see her, even in the dark?

The memory of what had happened four nights ago washed over her—Miriam, her sister, Sarah, and their mother lost in the North Georgia mountains. Wrongly, they'd thought the cops would provide help.

Her heart broke. Tears filled her eyes and her body ached, but she willed her legs forward. The farmhouse was her only hope.

She crossed the clearing and reached the house. Clutching the wood banister, she pulled herself up the stairs to the porch. Relief overcame her, along with exhaustion. Too spent to lift her hand to knock, she gasped when the door opened.

Warmth from inside washed over her. A tall, muscular man stood backlit in the threshold. "Help me," she pleaded, her head whirling. She grabbed his hand. "He... he wants to kill me."

Abram Zook reached for the frightened woman who fell into his arms. Her plaintive cry for help touched a broken place deep within him. Instinctively he pulled her close and cradled her to him.

His sister, Emma, limped down the stairs, wrapping a shawl around her bedclothes.

"Abram, why are you standing in the doorway at this time of night?"

Coming toward him, she gasped, seeing the woman in his arms. "*Gott* help us."

"*Gott* help this woman," Abram countered.

He carried her to the rocker near the wood-burning stove and gently placed her on the chair.

Emma retrieved the lantern from the table but stopped short when the screech of tires pulled her gaze to the still open doorway. "Abram, look."

He glanced to where his sister pointed, seeing headlights approaching much too fast along the icy road.

"Stay with the woman."

Emma reached for his arm. "You cannot save the *Englisch* from their foolish ways. Do not get involved."

He shrugged off her warning. "The bridge is out. I must alert the driver."

Abram stepped onto the porch. His eyes adjusted quickly to the dark night.

"Take the lantern," Emma insisted from the doorway.

Ignoring the request, he ran toward the road, flailing his arms to flag down the oncoming vehicle.

The car screeched to a stop. The driver lowered the window. Abram raised his hand to his eyes, unable to see the driver's face in the glare of the headlights.

"Did a car pass by here?" the man demanded, his voice as brittle as the ice on the roadway.

"The bridge is out. You must take the other fork in the road." Abram pointed to where the narrow country path split.

The man glanced back. "Did she go that way?"

Abram would not betray the woman he had cradled against him. "Your car is the first I have seen tonight."

Cursing, the man turned his vehicle around and screeched away from Abram. The back wheels spun on the slick pavement. He took the fork and accelerated.

Abram hurried back to the house.

Emma locked the door behind him. "Who was that man?" she asked.

"I do not know."

"He was looking for the woman." She stated what they both knew was true.

"Perhaps, but he will not find her tonight."

"I tell you, Abram, she will bring trouble to this house."

"She is in need, Emma. We will take her upstairs."

He lifted the woman into his arms and felt her startle. "I have you. You are safe."

She was thin, too thin.

His sister held the lantern aloft and climbed the stairs ahead of him. On the second floor she pushed open the door to the extra bedroom.

As Abram stepped past her, light from the lantern spilled over the woman's pale face. His sister inhaled sharply.

He glanced down, taking in the blood that spattered her clothing, the gash to her forehead and the scrapes to her hands and wrists.

His heart lurched.

What had happened to this woman on the run?

"You are awake?"

Miriam blinked her eyes open to daylight filtering through the window then turned her gaze to the man standing in the doorway of the small bedroom where she lay. He had a ruddy, wind-burned complexion with a dark beard and shaggy black hair that fell below his ears. His white shirt hugged his broad chest and puckered against the suspenders attached to his trousers.

Her mind slowly put the pieces together as she glanced from his clothing to the stark bedroom furnishings and back again to her larger-than-life rescuer. Was she dreaming or had she somehow, in the dead of night, found refuge in an Amish house?

Memories flashed through her mind. Struggling to put her thoughts in order, she tugged the quilt closer to her chin.

His brow knit. "You are afraid?"

Of him? Should she be?

She glanced behind the man to where a woman stood. Petite, with wide eyes and rosy cheeks, she wore a pale blue dress and white apron. Her hair was pulled into a bun under a starched cap. Miriam strained to remember, recalling only snippets of how the woman had tended her cut and dressed her in a flannel nightgown. At least that much she could recall.

The Amish man turned to the woman next to him. "Emma, she needs to eat."

Miriam shook her head. Food wasn't important. Being free of Serpent was all that mattered. Then, just that fast, her stomach rumbled, reminding her she hadn't had more than a few crackers in four days.

Gathering her courage, she swallowed hard and gave voice to the question that pinged through her head. "Who… who are you?"

"My name is Abram. We will talk soon."

He stepped into the hallway and pulled the door closed behind him.

"Wait," she called.

The door opened again. He stared at her, his face drawn, eyes pensive.

Was he friend or foe? She couldn't tell.

"My cell," she explained. "I need to make a phone call."

"I do not have your cell," he stated.

"But it was in my hand, then I dropped it into my pocket." She raised her voice for emphasis. "You have my clothes."

He glanced at the woman. He'd called her Emma. Was she his wife?

"You have found a phone?" he asked.

"No, Brother." The woman shook her head. "A phone was not among her clothing."

"That can't be right," Miriam objected. Why couldn't they both understand? "Do you know what a cell phone looks like?"

The man pursed his lips. His face clouded, either with anger or frustration. "My sister did not find a cell phone among your things."

"Do you have a phone? A landline? Or a computer with internet access?"

He raised his hand as if to silence her. "You must eat. Then we will talk." The door closed.

Miriam groaned with frustration. She threw off the covers, dropped her feet to the floor and sat upright. Her head throbbed and her mouth was thick as cotton. Gingerly, she touched her side, remembering the blow to her ribs.

Her muscles ached and the room swirled when she stood. Holding on to the wooden bedframe, she pulled back the sheer material that covered the window and glanced outside. In the distance she could see hills and a winding road, no doubt, the one she had raced along last night. She shivered, remembering her car careering over the embankment and heading for the icy water.

The muffled sound of a door slamming on the first floor forced her gaze to the yard below. The man left the house and walked with purposeful strides across the dormant winter grass. He had donned a black coat and felt hat with a wide brim and turned his head, left to right, as if to survey his land as he walked.

A crow cawed overhead. She strained to hear the sounds that usually filled her ears, of cars and sirens and train whistles. Here the quiet was as pristine as the landscape.

Glancing again at the man, she touched her hand to the windowpane, the cold glass taking her back four days.

A jumble of images flashed through her mind. The middle-of-the-night traffic stop on the mountain road. Two cops, one with the serpent tattoo insisting she leave her car. Her mother's confused outrage, escalating the situation until the second man stepped to the pavement and brandished his gun. The shots rang in her memory.

She closed her eyes, unwilling to go deeper into the tragedy. Instead she thought of her time at the cabin when she and her sister had been held captive.

Sarah!

Grief weighed upon her heart. Hot tears stung her eyes. Her sister, just barely twenty-one, had been carted away last night by a tall, skinny, red-haired man. His threat to silence Sarah if she didn't stop crying played through Miriam's mind and made her gasp with fear.

She choked back a sob of despair and wiped her hand over her cheeks, intent on regaining control of her emotions. She had escaped from the cabin. Now she had to find Sarah and learn the truth about her mother.

With a series of determined sniffs, she turned her focus back to the Amish man as he neared the barn and pulled the door open. He glanced over his shoulder. Then looked up. His gaze locked on hers.

Her cheeks burned. She dropped the curtain in place and stepped away from the window. She didn't want him to see her watching.

She had to get away, away from the mountains and back to civilization where she would find trustworthy officers who would enforce the law. Once they learned how she and her family had been attacked, they would hunt down the corrupt cops and help her find her sister.

She had to find Sarah. She had to find her alive.

TWO

"What do you want from me, Lord?" Abram had finished feeding the horses and now stared at the gray sky, wishing *Gott* would part the clouds and speak to his heart.

Bear trotted from the corner where he slept to rub against Abram's leg as if even the farm dog understood his confusion. Bending to rub Bear's neck, Abram took comfort in the animal's doleful gaze and desire to please.

"You are a smart dog, but you do not understand the human heart." Neither did Abram.

As Bear ambled back to his favorite corner, Abram straightened and stared again at the sky, questioning his own sensibilities. No woman had made him feel so much emotion since Rebecca. His first and only love had been taken too soon, which, as his faith told him, was *Gott*'s will. Although if that were true, then why in the dark moments of the night did he question *Gott*'s wisdom?

He turned his gaze to the second-story window where the woman had stood earlier. Abram had not learned her name, yet he yearned to know more about her. She had fallen into his arms, seeking help, not knowing of his failings in the past.

What had come over him, thinking thoughts about another woman? Especially an *Englisch* woman?

A righteous man lusted not with his eyes nor his heart.

The admonition sprang from deep within him, darkening his already somber outlook.

He left the barn and headed for the house, turning as a car pulled into his drive. The sheriff braked to a stop and crawled from his squad car. He was mid-fifties with graying hair and tired eyes that had lost their sparkle years earlier.

Abram approached the car and extended his hand. "Samuel."

The sheriff—Abram's uncle—smiled ruefully as the two men shook hands. "You're the only one in the family who acknowledges me, for which I'm grateful."

"*Yah*, but if you returned home to Ethridge, you might find some who would offer welcome."

"Your mother, perhaps. She is a good woman who knows how to forgive. I don't think your father would be as charitable."

Abram knew too well his father's unwillingness to forgive. "My father does not understand a man who leaves his faith."

"The Amish way was not my way. We have talked of this before." Samuel sniffed. "You're a good man to allow me into your life, Abram."

"I welcome you as the sheriff of Willkommen. You keep the peace so I can live in peace, as well."

He studied his uncle, seeing the shadows under his eyes and the flash of regret that could not be hidden. "Yet you still question your decision."

Samuel's brow furrowed. "What makes you think I'm not at peace?"

"I see it in the set of your jaw and the bent of your shoulders. You carry a heavy load."

"No heavier than you, my nephew. You still grieve for Rebecca."

"*Yah*, and for the mistake I made out of my own pride.

Not going to the *Englisch* hospital when her labor pains started cost Rebecca her life, as well as the life of our child. That is the burden I carry."

"And the bishop?"

"He says I am forgiven."

"Yet, what about you, Abram? Can you forgive yourself?"

The sheriff's eyes pierced the wall Abram had placed around his heart. Three years had passed but the wound was still so raw. A wound he feared would never heal.

Just like Emma's limp and his good friend Trevor's tragic death, some mistakes lasted forever.

"God doesn't exact payment for our wrongdoings, Abram. Remember that."

"My father would say you are wrong, Samuel."

"Does your father not have his own burdens?"

Abram smiled weakly. "I was his burden."

"Perhaps in your youth when you were struggling to find your way, but you remained Amish. That should have brought him comfort."

Longing to shift the conversation away from the past, Abram said, "You did not come here to talk about my transgressions."

"You're right." Samuel pointed to the mountain road. "Old Man Jacobs said two cars raced down the hill last night. Curtis Idler and my new deputy, Ned Quigley, are talking to him now and trying to get more information."

Abram turned his gaze to the road. "I am surprised Ezra Jacobs could see anything at night and even more surprised that he would contact the sheriff's office. As far as I know, he is one of the few *Englischers* who never installed a phone line."

"True, but his son, Walt, has been checking in on Ezra and left a cell for him to use in case he needed help."

"Did he need help last night?" Abram asked.

"Not help, but he was concerned." Samuel raised his

brow. "What about you, Abram? Did you see cars racing down the mountain?"

"Something has happened?"

"One of the cops in the next county found an abandoned car that ran off the road and nearly landed in the river. I'm headed there now. My deputies will join me when they finish talking to Jacobs."

"The mountain road can be slick and dangerous, yet you question me?"

"I thought you might have seen something. The car was found just over the county line and not far from your property."

How could Abram forget the man last night who was driving too fast?

"Besides, I had time to kill," the sheriff confessed. "Bruce Tucker, the chief of the Petersville Police Department, guards his turf like a bulldog. He'll insist his own officers search the scene before he invites me or any of my deputies on site."

Abram had heard talk about Tucker being less than cordial. "Chief Tucker does not welcome your help?"

"He does not want anyone's help. Some folks call him a *bensel*. Others say he is *schmaert* like a *hund*."

"A silly child or smart like a dog. You have not forgotten the language of your childhood, Samuel."

"I have not forgotten anything, Abram." Samuel frowned. "But you didn't answer my question. Did you see a car on the road last night?"

"*Yah.* The driver was going fast. I flagged him down and warned him about the bridge."

"Was anyone else in the car?"

"I saw only one person."

"Can you describe the driver?"

"The glare of headlights was in my eyes. He leaned out

the window, but I could not see his features. He turned the car around and took the fork in the road, heading west."

"What about the make of car and the license plate?" Samuel pressed.

"A black sedan. I did not think it was important to notice the license plate."

"Did you check the time?"

"Soon after midnight."

"Yet you were awake and saw his lights in time to warn him?" Samuel asked.

"Sleep is sometimes not my friend, as you must know."

His uncle glanced at the house. "What about Emma? Did she see anything?"

"Emma does not have trouble sleeping."

"Fortunate for her." The sheriff slapped Abram's shoulder in farewell before he returned to his car.

As he pulled onto the roadway, Abram climbed the steps of his porch and sighed deeply. He had to find out more about the woman upstairs.

He wanted to know who was after her and why.

Miriam stared at the tray of food Emma had brought to the guest bedroom. She had tried to eat, but her stomach was queasy and her mind kept flashing back to the smattering of details she could remember about the traffic stop.

In addition to the food, Emma had also provided a clean change of clothes—an Amish dress that she'd pulled from the blanket chest sitting in the corner of the room, along with an apron. Miriam considered herself a jeans-and-sweater type of gal, but the dress fit and she appreciated having something other than a flannel nightgown to wear.

Emma, probably mid-to-late twenties, was a foot shorter than Miriam with a pretty complexion and a sweet smile. She also exuded an abundance of patience as she showed Miriam how to straight-pin the dress at the bodice and waist. Working together, they had subdued Miriam's some-what unruly hair and twisted it into a bun.

Spying a number of skeins of yarn along with crochet hooks and knitting needles in the blanket chest and, know-ing she needed some outlet for the nervous energy that swelled within her, Miriam had asked if she could use the yarn to make a scarf for her newfound friend.

Emma seemed to appreciate the offer and her eyes spar-kled as she lumbered to the door. Miriam couldn't help but notice the deformed angle of her left foot that caused her to limp.

The Amish woman's handicap was obvious. Miriam clasped her hands to her heart, wondering about her own wounds, growing up within a dysfunctional family.

Maybe here in the quiet of this Amish home, she would quell the turmoil that had been the norm in her life for far too long. Then she thought of all that had happened and realized she was asking too much. Some scars cut too deep.

Sighing, she wrapped her arms around her waist and jerked when her finger snagged against the sharp tip of one of the straight pins. A bead of blood surfaced almost instantly. She glanced around the room, looking for a box of tissues. Seeing none, she neared the porcelain pitcher and washbowl on the oak dresser. After pouring water over her finger, she dried her hands on the thick towel and re-positioned the pin to prevent another prick.

Footsteps sounded, coming up the stairs. Her heart pounded, expecting Abram to open the door. Confusion had rocked her the last time he had done so. As much as she appreciated him giving her shelter for the night, she didn't want to face his penetrating eyes and stern gaze.

Miriam had seen the sheriff's car in the drive. Had Abram mentioned the woman hiding in his house?

The steps drew nearer. A knock at the door. "May I enter?"

His voice was deep, stilted. Did she detect an edge of impatience?

She wrung her hands to calm the trembling that came unbidden. What was wrong with her? She had done nothing wrong.

Again flashes of memories washed over her. Hot tears burned her eyes. She wiped at her cheeks, needing to be clear-headed and alert when she faced this giant of a man. No doubt he would question who she was and why she had stumbled into his life.

Another knock.

She stepped to the door and ever so slowly pulled it open. He stood on the other side, too close. Much too close.

Her breath hitched. She took a step back, needing to distance herself from his bulk and the smell of him that filled her nostrils with a mix of fresh soap and mountain air.

His hair, now neatly brushed back from his forehead, fell to where his beard hugged his square jaw, framing his face and accentuating the crystal blue of his eyes.

He dropped his gaze, taking in the simple dress she wore. Pain swept his face. He swallowed hard. "I will be downstairs. We need to talk." Without further explanation, he closed the door, his footsteps heavy as he descended the stairs.

She didn't want to talk to him. Not now. Not when so much had happened. If only she could find her cell phone. She needed to call Hannah. Her older sister had always known what she wanted, and it hadn't been to remain in Tennessee with a mother who showed the classic signs of early onset Alzheimer's.

Miriam needed help and someone to lean on for support.

Abram's broad shoulders came to mind.

She shook her head. She couldn't trust him. She couldn't trust any man, not even the Amish man who had saved her life.

THREE

Standing at the kitchen counter, Abram gulped down the last swig of coffee and wondered again about what had brought the mysterious woman to his door.

Should he have told Samuel? Her fear the night before had made Abram hesitant about revealing her presence. Thankfully his uncle had not asked him point-blank about the woman. Abram would not lie, but he need not divulge information that could terrorize her even more.

He placed the mug in the sink and rubbed his temple to still the pressure that had built up over the long hours he had tried to sleep. Seeing the woman wearing Rebecca's clothing had been a new stab to his heart. Of course, Emma had not realized the effect it would have on him.

The woman needed clothes to wear while her own things were being washed. His sister was shorter than their visitor, so offering Rebecca's dress had been a practical solution, except for what it had done to his equilibrium.

"You wanted to talk to me?"

He startled at the sound of the woman's voice and turned to face his guest. "I did not hear you come down the stairs."

His heart lurched again, seeing her in Rebecca's dress. He gripped the kitchen counter to steady himself and to make certain he was in the present and not dreaming of his wife yet with another face.

In an attempt to slow his racing heart, he searched for common ground. "The coffee is hot."

She shook her head. A strand of hair fell over her pale cheek. "I'm full from breakfast."

"Then you had enough to eat?"

"More than enough. I'm grateful for your hospitality."

"I do not know your name."

"Miriam," she quickly replied.

He waited, expecting more. Then, when she failed to respond, he raised his brow. "Should you not have a family name, as well?"

"Of course." Her face flushed. "It's Miller."

"Your father's name?"

"Actually, it was my mother's surname." She paused before adding, "My mother lived in Willkommen as a child. I was headed there to find her sister, but I got lost on the mountain roads. Is the town far?"

"Ten miles at most."

She took a step closer, her gaze expectant. "Then you might know Annie Miller."

"I know Eli Miller. His wife's name is Hattie. Perhaps your aunt has married?"

"I... I..." She faltered. "I don't know. My mother had only recently mentioned that she had a sister."

"You should ask more from your mother."

She wrung her hands. "I could call my sister if I had my phone."

"Could your phone have dropped from your pocket?" he offered, hoping to soothe her unease.

"Maybe. I'm not sure. What about a computer? I mentioned it upstairs, but you didn't answer me. Don't some Amish people use computers for business?"

"I do not have electricity to run a computer, nor a computer. That is not the way I live."

She held up her hand. "I didn't mean to offend you."

"I did not take your comment as an offense."

Her oval face was tight with worry. She rubbed her arms.

"You are cold?" he asked, concerned for her well-being.

"I'm fine, except I need my phone."

"There are phones in Willkommen. You can call from there."

She raised her hand to her forehand and carefully played her fingertips over the blackened bruise. "The problem is that I can't remember my sister's number. We haven't talked in…"

She shook her head and bit her lip as if she couldn't finish the thought that played heavy on her heart. "My sister's number is programmed in the contacts on my cell, that's why I need to find my phone."

"Perhaps you cannot remember her number because you are tired. You did not sleep well?"

She dropped her hand and bristled ever so slightly. "My problem is not lack of sleep."

He had pushed too far. Abram pointed to her forehead. "Someone hit you?"

"I fell," she corrected. "Your sister was kind enough to clean the wound last night."

A man had chased after her. A man who, according to her own words, wanted to kill her. A husband perhaps. Abram glanced at her left hand where he had not seen a ring as the *Englisch* were accustomed to wear. He did, however, see the bruise marks around her wrists.

Nervously she wiped her hands along the fabric of her dress. "Thank you for the clothing. It belongs to someone in your family? Your wife? She…" A furtive glance. "She is away?"

"My sister did not tell you?"

Innocent eyes. How could someone seemingly so open with her gaze be chased by a crazed man? He hesitated, weighing the thoughts that tangled through his mind.

"Tell me what, Abram?"

His chest tightened at the inflection of her voice when she said his given name.

"I'm sorry," she quickly added.

Had she noticed his surprise?

"Is it impolite to use your first name?" she asked. "I don't know Amish customs nor your last name."

"Zook. My name is Abram Zook. My wife, Rebecca, and my unborn child died three years ago."

Miriam's face clouded as if feeling his pain. "I'm sorry, Mr. Zook, and I apologize for any impropriety on my part." She touched the bodice of the dress Rebecca had so carefully stitched.

The front panel had challenged his wife when the fabric refused to lay straight. The memory of her bright smile when she had mastered the problem brought heaviness to his heart. The dress had been the last she had made before learning she was with child.

He turned, unable to face the woman in his wife's clothing. Instead he stared through the kitchen window. His gaze took in the hillside and the winding road that had brought the *Englisch* woman to his door.

"I've upset you after you were nice enough to take me in." She sighed. "As soon as I have my phone, I'll be on my way."

Slowly he turned to face her, needing to gauge her reaction to his next statement. "The sheriff said a car ran off the road, not far from here, but in the next county."

Fear clouded her eyes. She rubbed her neck and glanced down. "Did…did you tell the sheriff about me?"

"He did not ask if I had visitors so I did not tell him."

She glanced up, her gaze a swirl of unrest. "I haven't done anything wrong."

"I did not think you had." He hesitated a long moment

before adding, "Yet a man followed you last night. He is your husband?"

Shock—no, horror—washed over her pale face. "I would never have anything to do with an animal like him."

"Yet he was looking for you."

She raised her chin. "I ask that you trust me. I'm innocent of any wrongdoing, but the man is evil. I don't want you or your sister to get involved. That's why I have to leave. Now. Can you take me to Willkommen? From there, I can catch a bus to Atlanta."

"I will take you to Willkommen, but not today." Not while law enforcement in two counties was investigating an abandoned car. For her own safety, the woman needed to stay put.

"But I have to contact my older sister in Atlanta."

He nodded. "You can do so when we go to town tomorrow."

She took a step back. Frustration clouded her gaze. "What will I do until then?"

The back door opened and Emma stepped inside, carrying a basket of apples. She glanced questioningly at Miriam and then at her brother.

He lifted his hat off the wall peg and stepped toward the open door. "Our guest wishes to help you."

His sister's face darkened. "Where are you going, Abram?"

"The fence needs repair. Lock the door after I am gone."

Emma caught his arm. "You are worried that the sheriff will return?"

"I am not worried." He stepped onto the porch.

"You did not eat this morning, Abram," his sister called after him. "You will be hungry."

"I will survive."

"*Yah.* You are a strong man."

Before the door closed he heard Emma's final comment. "Perhaps too strong."

His sister knew his weakness almost as well as he knew it himself.

"Gott," he mumbled, looking up at the sky and shaking his head with regret. "Forgive me for my prideful heart."

"Wait!" Miriam hurried past a startled Emma and grabbed a black cape off the hook by the door. Throwing it around her shoulders, she raced from the house.

"Abram," she called.

Surprise registered on his square face as he turned. Or was it impatience? With his pensive gaze and stoic expression, the man was hard to read.

"I need your help," she said, running toward him.

He hesitated a moment, probably thinking of the fence that demanded his attention.

"You're right about my phone." Miriam stopped short of where he stood. "It must have fallen from my pocket."

She looked at the winding mountain road in the distance and the grassy pasture that led toward a thick wood. "But, I'm confused. Do you know the direction I would have walked last night? I remember coming through the woods, then a clearing."

"The sheriff mentioned a car bogged in mud at the river's edge." Abram pointed to the stand of trees at the far side of the pasture. "The county line is just beyond those pines that mark the end of my property. The river curves close to the road there. I believe it is where you left your car."

Overwhelmed by the vast area she would have to cover, Miriam pulled in a deep breath and nodded with resolve. "I'll start by looking around the house first."

"You have heard the saying, 'a needle in a haystack'?"

The seriousness of his tone made her smile. "Does that mean I should give up before I start?"

His full lips twitched and a spark of levity brightened his gaze. "We will search together. I will help you, Miriam."

She liked the way he said her name as well as his offer of assistance. Returning his almost smile with one of her own, she felt a huge weight lift off her shoulders. "Thank you, Abram."

"We will begin here." He pointed to the stepping stones upon which they stood. "And we will take the path through the pasture. Perhaps you followed it last night."

Without further delay he dropped his gaze and walked slowly toward the drive. Miriam followed close behind him, searching the winter grass cut short enough that a cell phone would be visible.

On the far side of the dirt drive she paused and breathed in the serenity of the setting, then smiled as a big dog with long, golden hair ambled out of the barn. She patted her hand against her thigh, calling him closer. "What's the pup's name?"

Abram stopped to watch the dog sidle next to Miriam. "His name is Bear."

She rubbed behind the dog's ear. "You're big as a bear, but sweet." She cooed to the dog before looking up at Abram. "He's part golden retriever?"

"With a mix of Lab."

Again she lowered her gaze to the dog. "How come I haven't seen you before this?" Bear wagged his tail and nuzzled closer as if enjoying the attention.

"He sleeps in the barn. You did not see him last night because I had closed the doors to keep the horses warm."

"I'm glad I got to meet you today, Bear." With a final pat to the dog's head, Miriam straightened and took in the pristine acreage around Abram's house. In the distance, a number of horses grazed on the hillside. "The animals are yours?"

"*Yah.* The others are in the barn." A look of pride and accomplishment wrapped around his handsome face. "Horses are necessary for the Amish way of life. They provide transportation. They pull our plows and haul produce and products to market."

"They're beautiful, but a car and tractor would make your life easier."

"Easier does not mean better." He returned to his search, leaving her to ponder his statement.

So many people yearned for modern conveniences to enhance their quality of life. But did possessions bring contentment?

Her mother had traveled the country, looking for happiness. Instead she had found unrest and confusion.

In her youth Miriam had longed for a father to love her and the security of a stable home. She had found neither.

Like the elusive memories of her past, the wind tugged at the hem of her dress and wrapped the fabric around her legs. For a fleeting moment she felt a new appreciation for the Amish way and almost a kinship with this man who embraced the simple life.

Hurrying to catch up to Abram, she asked, "What can you tell me about the sheriff? He's from Willkommen?"

"Originally he came from Tennessee. His name is Samuel Kurtz. He is my mother's brother."

Not what she had expected to hear. "The sheriff is your uncle?"

Abram studied the surprise she was hard-pressed to control. "Does that seem strange to you?" he asked.

"A bit." Actually it surprised her a lot. "How can an Amish man work in law enforcement?"

"Before baptism, young men and women decide how they will live their lives, whether they will remain in the community or move elsewhere. My uncle did not wish to remain Amish. Our family is from Ethridge, Tennessee. Samuel came to Georgia to make a new life for himself. He is respected here. A year ago, he was elected sheriff."

"You moved here to be near your uncle?"

"The land brought me. The price was good. I wanted to make a new home for myself and my wife."

"Did you ever consider leaving the Amish way, like your uncle?"

"Once, but I was young and foolish. Thankfully, I changed my mind and realized what I would be leaving." His eyes softened. "The Amish walk a narrow path, Miriam, but we know where it leads. My uncle wanted something else for his life."

"And he's happy?" she quizzed.

"You will have to ask him." Abram motioned her toward a path that cut across the pasture. "This is the way you walked last night."

She glanced back at the house. "How can you be so certain?"

"Your footprint is there in the dirt."

Glancing at where he pointed, she recognized the faint outline of her shoe.

"Which means we don't have to search the entire pasture to find my cell." Feeling a swell of relief, Miriam hurried forward, hoping her phone would be as easy to find as her footprint.

Abram led the way, seemingly intent on the quest, until the sound of a motor vehicle turned his gaze to the road.

"A car is coming," he warned. "You must go back to the house."

She wasn't ready to give up the search. "I haven't found my cell."

He took her arm, his grasp firm, and turned her around. "Hurry. Someone comes."

The intensity of his tone drove home the danger of being seen. Fear overcame her and she ran toward the house. Was she running for protection or running into a trap?

Everything inside Abram screamed that he had to protect Miriam. From what or from whom, he was not sure.

He ran to the road and stepped onto the pavement just as the Willkommen sheriff's car rounded the bend. Abram glanced back at the pasture. Miriam was still running, the black cape billowing out behind her.

His heart thumped a warning for her and one for himself, as well. His actions since Miriam had stumbled onto his porch were so outside the norm that it seemed as if someone else had taken control of his body and his mind.

Seeing his uncle at the wheel of the squad car, Abram raised his hand in greeting. Samuel slowed the vehicle to a stop and rolled down the window. Abram leaned into the car.

His uncle's face was drawn, his eyes filled with sadness.

"Go home, Abram, and lock your doors." Samuel flicked his gaze to the fleeing figure in the distance. "Keep Emma inside."

Thankfully, his uncle had not questioned Miriam's even gait and, instead, had mistaken the *Englischer* for his sister.

Knowing something serious was underfoot, Abram pressed for more information. "What is it you are trying to tell me, Samuel?"

"I mentioned that the Petersville police found a car at the river's edge. When I got there, they were searching the back seat and taking prints. They found a woman's purse."

"The handbag belongs to the person who owns the car?"

The sheriff nodded but the pull of his jaw told Abram more than a purse was at stake.

"The trunk of the car was locked. They were preparing to break it open when I left."

A nerve twitched in Abram's jaw. A roar filled his ears. He strained to hear the sheriff's words.

"The car is registered to a woman, age twenty-four. The police are trying to track her down."

Emma's warning about Miriam floated again through Abram's mind. *She will bring trouble to this house.*

What had become of the peace and surety of his life? Overnight he had gone from calm to chaos.

"The woman who owns the car is from a small town outside Knoxville," Samuel continued. "One of Chief Tucker's officers contacted the authorities there. Seems she lived with her mother and younger sister. All three women have been missing for a number of days. No one knows where they went. The daughter told the neighbors her mother had Alzheimer's, yet the neighbors claimed the mother seemed normal."

Miriam had not mentioned her mother's dementia.

"The younger sister's twenty-one." The sheriff tugged on his jaw. "She's missing, as well."

"What are you saying, Samuel?"

"I'm saying you need to be on guard, Abram. Deputy Idler will stop by once they learn what's in the trunk. I wanted him to alert you and the other Amish families who live out here if anything points to foul play. The circumstances are different, but I keep thinking about Rosie Glick, that Amish girl who went missing some months ago."

"Supposedly, Rose ran off with an *Englisch* boy."

"That's what we thought at the time. Now I'm not so sure."

Abram could no longer keep silent. "There is something I need to tell you, Samuel, that might tie—"

Glancing at his watch, the sheriff held up his hand to cut Abram off. "It'll have to wait. I've got to get back to town. Art Garner, one of my deputies, was involved in a vehicular accident on the road leading up Pine Lodge

Mountain. He's being air-evacuated to Atlanta. I told his wife I'd drive her to the hospital."

"You will return tomorrow?"

The sheriff shook his head. "I need to handle some business while I'm in the city and won't be back for at least three days. The Petersville police will be in charge of the investigation. Idler will be the point of contact on our end. He'll keep you updated if new information surfaces."

The sheriff narrowed his gaze. "Be careful, Abram. Watch your back until the women are found."

"But, Samuel—" Before Abram could mention his houseguest, the sheriff pulled his sedan onto the roadway and sped down the hill, taking the fork in the road that headed to Willkommen.

Tension tightened Abram's spine as he gazed at his house in the distance. Miriam had come back out of the house and was standing on the porch, tugging at her hair. Was she fearful of what the sheriff had found?

Slowly he walked toward her. In his mind, he laid out the many questions he needed to ask. Before he reached the drive, the sound of another car cut through the stillness.

"Go inside, Miriam," he called. "Now."

Her eyes widened, but thankfully she complied and closed the door behind her just as one of the Willkommen deputy's cars pulled into the drive.

Curtis Idler, midforties with a muscular build and receding hairline, climbed from the passenger side and nodded to Abram. He pointed to a second deputy behind the wheel. "You know Ned Quigley?"

"We have never met, but Samuel has mentioned his name." Abram bent and peered into the squad car. Ned was probably ten years younger than Idler, but a big man with full cheeks and curly hair. The deputy raised his hand in greeting. Abram nodded before turning his focus to Idler.

A scowl covered the older deputy's drawn face and angled jaw. "I came to warn you, Abram. A woman, probably midfifties, was shot twice. Her body was locked in the trunk of the car that was abandoned by the river. Looks like she's been dead a few days. Thankfully she was zipped up tight in a plastic mattress bag or you would have smelled her even here."

Abram's stomach soured at the thought of the dead woman jammed into the trunk of a car.

Idler pulled a smartphone from his pocket. He tapped on the cell a number of times and then angled the screen so Abram could see the picture that came into view.

"I know you Amish are against photography, but you need to see this."

As much as Abram did not want to look at the phone, his eyes were drawn there.

"The murdered woman's name is Leah Miller. She's from Tennessee. This is the suspect we're looking for," the deputy continued. "A killer who's considered armed and dangerous."

Abram's heart lurched as he stared at the photo.

A killer? Armed and dangerous?

Something was terribly wrong.

Abram fought to control his emotions as Idler climbed into the passenger seat and Quigley backed the car out of the drive.

All Abram could see was the photo on Idler's phone.

The photo was of Miriam.

Miriam was not a killer. Or was she?

FOUR

Miriam stood next to the woodstove, but even with the warmth from the burning logs she felt chilled to the core. Her hands shook as she shoved hair back from her face and braced herself for Abram's reproach.

Emma washed apples in the kitchen sink, her back to Miriam, for which she was grateful. The woman's silence was indication enough of the tension that filled the house.

Abram's heavy footfalls on the porch signaled his approach before the door opened and he stepped across the threshold. He glanced at Miriam with hooded blue eyes then he spoke to his sister in what must have been Pennsylvania Dutch from the harsh guttural sounds Miriam couldn't understand.

Emma nodded curtly and scurried out of the kitchen and up the stairs, leaving Miriam to wrap her arms tightly around her midriff and pull in a deep breath. She was determined to stand her ground against the tall and muscular man whose presence sucked the air from her lungs.

Serpent had warned her about other police officers working with him. He'd insisted that alerting law enforcement would cause Miriam more harm than good.

"I do not know what the sheriff told you," she said, taking the offensive before Abram could accuse her. She spread her hands. "As I mentioned to you earlier, I have done nothing wrong."

"You are quick to rationalize behavior about which I have not spoken."

Gathering courage from deep within, she refused to lower her gaze. "I will leave as soon as possible," she said through tight lips. "But I need my clothing and my phone. I also need transportation to Willkommen. As I mentioned earlier, I presume there is a bus that will take me to Atlanta."

"Yah." He nodded. "The bus runs at the end of the week."

"Do you know the schedule?"

He shook his head. "But you can check when we are in town."

"If you drop me at the bus station, I can—"

What would she do without money? Somewhere along the way, she'd lost her purse, although she kept an emergency stash of fifty-dollar bills in the glove compartment of her car. Hopefully the police wouldn't flip through the pages of the vehicle maintenance book where she had hid the money.

Abram was staring at her.

"I'll be safe with my sister, Hannah, in Atlanta," she said, trying to pick up her train of thought.

"The person you hoped to call with your phone?"

Miriam nodded. "That's right."

"Still you do not remember her phone number?"

"The number is programmed in the contacts on my phone," Miriam explained. "I told you all this earlier."

He raised a brow. "Yet you told me nothing about your mother."

She took a step back. "My mother?"

Miriam's cheeks burned. She didn't need a mirror to realize how hot and flushed she must look.

Abram pointed to the kitchen table. "It is time we talk freely."

He indicated the bench where he wanted her to sit. She lowered herself onto the long wooden seat and remained silent as he sat across from her.

The table was smooth as silk and gleamed with shellac or polish or a mix of both. She glanced at his large hands, noting the scrapes and calluses, realizing he had probably made the table.

Serpent's hands were soft with short, pudgy fingers. What he lacked in size, he made up for with brute force.

She cringed, remembering the strike to her forehead and the jab to her ribs. Without thinking, she touched the tender spot at the side of her brow.

Abram's eyes followed her hand. "Who hurt you?"

She could no longer hide the truth. "A policeman who has a serpent tattooed on his neck."

"You stayed with him?"

"Not willingly."

Abram flattened his palms on the table. "Why do you hesitate telling me your story?"

"My story?" Did he think this was make-believe?

"What happened, Miriam? Why were you with him? Why do you have bruises on your wrists?"

Unwilling to relive the experience, she started to rise. Abram caught her hand. His touch was firm, yet gentle, and his gaze was filled with understanding.

She stared at him for a long moment, searching for any sign of aggression. All she saw was compassion and a concern for her well-being.

Pulling in a ragged breath, she lowered herself onto the bench. She had nowhere else to turn and no one, other than this Amish man, to help her. She would have to trust him with her *story*, as he called it. He had taken her in and he deserved to know the truth about what had happened on the mountain.

Her mouth was dry, her throat tight. She pulled her hand free from his hold and toyed with her fingers, weighing how to begin.

"I… I lived in Tennessee with my mother and younger sister, Sarah. My older sister moved to Atlanta a few years ago."

"Hannah?" he asked.

"That's right. She's two years older than I am." Miriam paused, struggling for a way to explain the reality of her life. "Our mother was a free spirit of sorts."

She glanced at Abram. "Do you understand that term?"

The faintest hint of a smile curled his full lips. "Although the Amish end their formal education at the eighth grade, there is much that can be learned outside the schoolhouse."

"I didn't mean to imply that you weren't educated. I just wasn't sure if you had heard of the expression."

"You said your mother was a free spirit." He brought her back to the subject at hand.

Miriam wiped her fingers over the tabletop, wishing her life had been as smooth. "Mother carted us across the United States. We rarely stayed for more than a few months in any one place."

Thinking back to her youth, Miriam shook her head. "We were pulled out of so many schools. We longed for a normal life. We had anything but stability, living with our mother."

"How did you get to Tennessee?"

"Friends invited Mother to visit. They had a small home for rent outside of Knoxville, and we moved in. Not long after that she started showing signs of dementia. I took her to a local doctor who diagnosed her with early onset Alzheimer's. You're aware of the condition?"

Abram nodded. "I am."

"Her mind slowly deteriorated."

"Yet you brought her to Georgia?" he asked.

"Which is what she wanted, although in hindsight we never should have left Knoxville."

"But you always did what your mother wanted."

"Which now sounds foolish and immature." She hung her head, thinking of the real reason she had agreed to travel to Georgia. Abram didn't need to know her motives. She'd made a horrific mistake, one that would haunt her for the rest of her life.

"A few months ago," Miriam continued, "Mother started talking about an estranged sister with whom she hoped to reconnect."

"This is the aunt who lives in Willkommen?"

Nodding, Miriam added, "Annie Miller is her name, although I'm not sure where she lives or if she even exists. Mother became insistent that she needed to see her sister. Prior to that, she had never talked about her family or siblings, and we never brought up the subject."

A sigh escaped Miriam's lips. "Knowing it was a subject she didn't want to talk about kept us from asking questions. We knew her parents had died and that she'd rejected their faith."

Abram's eyes widened ever so slightly. "Your mother did not believe in *Gott*?"

"She believed there was a God, she just didn't believe she needed Him in her life. Or that we needed Him. We lived near San Antonio for a period of time and visited a few of the missions. I saw something there that I wanted in my own life. A love of God. An ability to turn to Him in times of need. A belief in His goodness and mercy."

"Did you tell your mother how you felt?" Abram asked.

"I tried. She became agitated and insisted I was being foolish. We moved not long after that."

"Which made you even more hesitant to discuss faith."

Miriam's heart warmed. "That's it exactly. To maintain peace and some semblance of family stability, we skirted any mention of the Lord."

"And now?" He raised his brow.

She was puzzled by his question. "I don't understand."

"How do you feel about *Gott* now?"

"I..." She tried to identify her feelings. "I'm not sure. I started attending a church in Tennessee when Mother's condition grew worse. I was searching, maybe reaching out for help. The people were welcoming, but I struggled to accept the fullness of their faith in God. Perhaps I had pushed Him aside too many times."

Turning her gaze to the window, she could see the horses grazing on the hillside. "I doubt the Lord would have interest in a woman who grew up fearing to mention His name."

"You were young, Miriam. You had no one to teach you or lead you to faith. Besides, *Gott* would not hold you accountable for the actions of your mother."

"I don't know if that's true, Abram. I worked in a local craft shop and tried to earn enough money to pay the rent and put food on the table. I didn't need to compound my struggle with issues of faith."

She offered him a weak smile. "We've gotten off topic. You wanted to know about Serpent."

Painful though it was to give voice to the flashes of clarity that circled through her mind, she slowly and methodically explained, as best she could, the middle-of-the-night traffic stop that turned tragic.

"I was driving. It was late and the mountain roads confused me. Seeing the police lights in my rearview mirror brought relief, until I saw the serpent tattoo on the neck of the so-called officer. He made me leave the car. My mother became agitated. She lunged from the back seat, screaming, and rushed at him with raised fists. A second guy remained inside the police vehicle. I had the feeling he was in charge and that Serpent was doing his bidding."

"Can you describe him?"

"I wish I could. The flashing light on the roof of the car blinded me. When my mother went after Serpent, the other guy stepped to the pavement and turned his weapon on her. He fired once, twice. I didn't see his face. All I saw was my mother's blood."

Hot tears burned her eyes. "I… I don't know what happened after that. Sarah was still in the car. I struggled to get to her. Serpent struck me and knocked me out. I never saw my mother again."

The tight expression that washed over Abram's face chilled her. "What have you learned?" she demanded, anticipating the answer before he spoke.

He took her hand. "The police found an older woman's body in the trunk of your car."

Miriam dropped her head and moaned. She had feared her mother was dead, but hearing the words spoken was like a knife piercing her heart.

Abram circled the table and slid next to her on the bench. His muscular arms wrapped around her and pulled her into his embrace.

For so many years she had longed for strong shoulders to support her. Never had she suspected comfort would come from an Amish man whose upbringing and background were so totally different from hers.

She buried her head against his chest and cried heart-wrenching sobs for all that had happened. For the trip to Georgia that had ended in tragedy. For Sarah, who had been taken and might never be found again. And for the horrific murder of the mother Miriam had loved so much, who had never loved her in return.

"I will not let this man hurt you again," Abram whispered as he gathered Miriam deeper into his embrace.

As much as he wanted her to remain there, she eventually pulled back. Her face was blotched with tears, but even then he saw her determination to muster on.

She sniffed and wiped her hands over her cheeks. "There's more to tell, Abram."

He relaxed his hold on her, knowing she needed space.

She dabbed at her eyes and bit her lip. Then, playing her fingers over the smooth finish of the table, she drew in series of jagged breaths and straightened her spine as if gathering courage and finding the wherewithal to continue.

"Serpent—" Her voice was raspy and little more than a whisper when she finally spoke. "Serpent took my sister and me to a cabin. I heard water. We could have been near the river. He tied each of us up in different rooms. I was worried about Sarah, but no matter how hard I struggled, I couldn't get free."

She swallowed hard. "I… I pretended to be asleep when he checked on me. When light filtered through the window the next morning, he forced me to swallow a pill. I spit it out, but he struck me and said he would kill Sarah if I didn't take the drug. I pretended to do so and then coughed it up when he left the room. The next time, I wasn't as lucky. He clamped my jaw closed until the pill dissolved in my mouth."

Abram could only imagine the terror both Miriam and her sister had experienced. A rage against the two men grew within him.

"Days passed in a blur," she said, her voice growing stronger. "I heard snippets of conversations. Some on the phone… One night a guy with a deep voice stopped by. I overheard just a portion of what they said. They kept mentioning *trafficking* and *women*. The night I escaped, another man came to the cabin. I saw him through the window. He was tall and skinny with red hair. He hauled Sarah away and Serpent said he was going to dispose of her."

Abram took her hand and was relieved when she squeezed his fingers.

"When Serpent came to give me more drugs, I didn't respond. He probably thought I was still sedated. Later, after what seemed like hours, I broke free from the rope that had held me. He had become complacent and had forgotten to attach the cord to the bedposts. I slipped outside and found the key to my car on the floorboards. He must have heard the engine start because he ran from the cabin before I pulled onto the main road."

"But you escaped, Miriam."

She nodded. "I was crazy with fear and so tired. I hid in the woods, but he found me and chased me. One of my tires had a blowout and my car almost ended up in the river. Somehow I got out and started running. Then I saw the light in your window."

"*Gott* led you here."

"I… I was worried when I saw you talking to the sheriff. Serpent said he would pin my mother's death on me. He said all the cops in this area were working together with him. He said they would believe his story."

"What he claimed has proven true, Miriam. Curtis Idler, the Willkommen deputy, said the police are searching for you. They suspect you killed your mother. Yet I do not understand how they could believe such an evil man with the serpent on his neck. He cannot be an officer of the law."

"But his car had a flashing light and a sign that read Petersville Police Department."

"The chief of police in Petersville is not to be trusted, so perhaps this Serpent, as you call him, is working with law enforcement, after all. I know my uncle will help you."

"Then I must tell him what happened."

Abram shook his head. "Samuel is traveling to Atlanta and will be gone for three days."

"I can't wait that long." Miriam's voice was insistent. "Serpent needs to be stopped now, before he hurts anyone else."

Emma hurried into the kitchen and stared at both of them. "Forgive me. I thought you had finished talking."

"You are right, my sister. We have finished our conversation." Abram released hold of Miriam's hand and stood. "Tomorrow we will go to Willkommen."

"But—"

"Tomorrow, Miriam. Until then, you will stay with Emma and me."

FIVE

Miriam shook her head with frustration as she thought about what terrible things could have befallen her sister. She needed to find Sarah as quickly as possible.

"You are upset with my brother," Emma said, drawing close. She placed a comforting hand on Miriam's shoulder. "He is worried about your well-being."

"Did you hear that the Petersville police suspect me of killing my own mother?"

Emma nodded and pointed to the small holes drilled through the ceiling. "The heat from the stove rises to warm the bedrooms. Abram's voice travels, as well. I tried not to listen, but I could not help but overhear what he said to you."

Miriam gazed into Emma's blue eyes, not nearly as crystal clear as her brother's but bright and filled with understanding. "How could they think I would do that? There is no evidence."

"Except this man who held you captive. You do not know the lies he has told."

Pulling in a ragged breath, Miriam fought the tears that welled up. She wiped her hand over her face and struggled to control her upset. "I'm usually not this fragile."

Emma raised her chin and smiled. "I see strength when

I look at you, Miriam. Not weakness. That is why you and Abram butt together. He is not used to a woman who speaks her mind."

"Am I that demanding?" she asked.

"Demanding is not the word I would use. You see things one way. Abram sees them another way. Soon, you will learn to work together."

"We could work together if he would take me to Willkommen."

"But what good would it do if the Petersville police arrest you?"

Emma patted Miriam's shoulder.

"Those who want to do you harm and those who suspect you of a crime would not think to find you here," the Amish woman continued. "You must remain hidden from view. Abram is a man of his word. Tomorrow, he will take you to Willkommen."

The *clip-clop* of a horse's hooves sent both women to peer out the window. Emma grabbed Miriam's hand when Abram appeared, guiding the horse and buggy to the back porch. "It seems my brother has changed his mind."

Miriam squeezed Emma's hand and then opened the door before Abram climbed the stairs to the back porch.

"We're going to town?" she asked, her heart overflowing with gratitude.

"*Yah.* Nellie is hitched and waiting. We will talk to Samuel's deputy, Curtis Idler. If my uncle left him in charge, then we can trust him."

"You both must be careful," Emma cautioned. "What if this Serpent is prowling about?"

"Hopefully he won't look for a woman in Amish clothing," Miriam said.

"Wear my bonnet." Emma pulled the wide-brimmed hat

from the wall peg. The shape reminded Miriam of what pioneer women wore to the keep the sun off their faces.

"We must hurry." Abram removed the black cape from a second peg and wrapped the heavy wool around Miriam's shoulders. Emma helped tie the bonnet under her chin.

"There is a blanket in the buggy if you are cold." He opened the door wider. "We will leave now."

Miriam's heart raced, knowing she could be in danger. At least Abram would be with her.

He helped her into the buggy. "Sit in the rear," he suggested. "You will be out of sight there."

She crawled onto the second seat and nodded to Emma as the horse started on the journey to town.

Abram sat in the front, the reins in his hands and his focus on the road.

Was Miriam making a good decision? Or would she regret leaving the refuge of Abram's home?

Abram's neck felt like a porcupine with his nerve endings on alert. With each breath, his muscles tensed even more as he sensed a looming danger, although he did not know from where the danger would come.

Maybe he was being foolish to leave the security of his home and travel to town. Out in the open, anything could happen.

He flicked his gaze over his shoulder to Miriam. Her eyes were wide, her face drawn. She clasped her hands as if in prayer and looked like a typical Amish woman with her black cape and bonnet. Then her gaze turned to him and a bolt of current coursed through him, as palpable as the lightening that looked ready to cut through the darkening sky.

Why did this woman—this *Englisch* woman—affect him so?

He turned his focus back to the road and lifted the reins ever so slightly. Nellie always responded to the slightest movement of his wrists and today was no exception. The mare increased her pace, the sound of her hooves on the pavement as rhythmic as a heartbeat.

Abram eyed the darkening sky. If only they could outrun the rain that seemed imminent. A harbinger of what would come?

"The day is turning dark," Miriam said from the rear. "What happens if it storms?"

"Sometimes we find shelter. Today we will continue on." Although, he knew Nellie could be skittish if lightning hit too close and thunder exploded around them. He would not share his concern with Miriam. From the tension he heard in her voice, she was worried enough.

Approaching a bend in the road, Abram pulled back on the reins and slowed Nellie's pace. He wanted to ensure nothing suspicious appeared ahead of them as they rounded the curve. His gut tightened when he spied police cars in the distance swarmed around a buggy. His pulse thumped a warning and his throat went dry.

"What is it, Abram?" Miriam leaned forward. Her hand touched his shoulder.

"A roadblock. There are a number of Petersville police cars and a deputy's car from Willkommen. It appears they are searching a buggy."

"What can we do?" she asked, her voice faltering.

He yanked on the reins. Nellie made a U-turn in the roadway and began retracing the route they had taken.

"The Petersville police suspect you murdered your mother. We must return home."

Moments later a car engine sounded behind them. Abram glanced around the side of the buggy. A black sedan with a flashing light on the roof was racing toward them.

"We are being followed. The car looks like the one I saw the night you escaped."

"It's Serpent."

Once they rounded the bend, Abram steered the buggy to the edge of the road and pulled back on the reins.

"You must hide." He pointed to a thicket. "There, in the woods."

Miriam crawled to the front of the buggy and held Abram's outstretched hand as she climbed to the pavement.

"Hurry," he warned. "Go deep into the woods. Find cover there."

Abram's heart pounded as he watched her flee, knowing he had made a terrible mistake. They never should have left the security of his house.

The black sedan raced around the bend and pulled to a stop. A man dressed in a navy shirt and khaki pants stepped to the pavement. He slapped Nellie's flank as he approached Abram.

"What is it you want?" Abram asked.

The man wore a scarf around his neck. Although muscular, he had small eyes with drooping upper lids, flattened cheeks and a short, upturned nose. His mouse-brown hair was thin on top but long on the sides.

"Why'd you turn your buggy around?" he demanded.

Abram pointed to the sky. "The clouds are dark. Rain is in the air. I do not wish to drench my buggy, my horse or my clothing."

The man stepped closer and peered past Abram into the rear of the carriage. "Someone was with you?"

"As you can see," Abram tried to assure him, "I am alone."

The man turned his gaze to the forest. He took a step forward. "There. I see movement." Just that fast, he ran toward the thicket exactly where Miriam had gone moments earlier.

Abram hopped from the buggy and started to follow.

A second car, this one from the Willkommen sheriff's office, pulled up behind the black sedan.

"Abram, stop."

He turned, spotting Ned Quigley, the newly hired sheriff's deputy.

"Did you see the guy driving the black sedan?" the deputy asked.

Abram beckoned him forward. "He ran into the woods."

"Stay with your buggy," Quigley said. "I'll find Pearson."

Pearson. Evidently Serpent had a name.

Abram ignored Quigley. He would never stay put when Miriam was in danger.

He pushed through the bramble. The deputy followed close behind.

Pulling in a ragged breath, Abram searched the forest. He had to find Miriam. He had to find her before Serpent did.

Miriam's heart nearly exploded in her chest, seeing Serpent follow her into the woods.

She couldn't outrun him, but where could she hide?

Her breath hitched and a roar filled her ears, nearly drowning out his footfalls as he trampled through the underbrush.

Overhead thunder rolled and the forest darkened with the encroaching storm.

A lump filled her throat and she struggled to keep the tears at bay. She couldn't cry. Not now, not when she needed to outsmart the snake that was so heinous.

More footsteps sounded. How many men were searching for her?

Abram had been right. She should have stayed undercover at his farmhouse instead of throwing herself into harm's way. More thunder rumbled as ominous as the situation she was in.

A cluster of rocks was visible through the pines. Would they provide a hiding spot?

Carefully she picked her way through the bramble, averting the twigs and branches that would snap if she stepped on them. Any sound would alert Serpent.

She gulped for air, her lungs constricting with the tension that made her hands shake and her heart lurch.

Careful though she tried to be, her foot snagged on a root. She toppled forward and caught herself just before she landed in a pile of dried leaves. Thankfully, at that very instant, a bolt of lightning crashed overhead and a blast of thunder covered the sound of her fall.

Regaining her footing, she scurried behind the rocks, willing herself to meld into the outcrop of granite. The skies opened and rain fell in fat drops that pinged against the rocks, the trees and the floor of the forest.

A deep guttural roar sounded, like a wild beast's bellow. Serpent was standing only a few feet away on the other side of the rock, venting his anger. If only he would be deterred from coming closer.

More footsteps. Her heart nearly ricocheted out of her chest. She flattened her hands and cheek against the granite trying to disappear into the stone.

"I know you're here." Serpent's voice, laced with fury.

Could he hear her heart beating uncontrollably in her chest?

"Pearson?" another voice called, deep and demanding.

Serpent grumbled.

"There he is." Abram's voice.

Relief swept over Miriam.

"You're on a wild-goose chase," the first man said as he drew closer.

"I saw something," Serpent replied.

The deep-voiced man snickered. "You saw that skunk standing at your backside."

"What!" Serpent groaned.

The putrid and unmistakable stench of a skunk's spray filled the air.

Leaves rustled wildly, followed by the sound of footsteps racing back to the roadway.

"Looks like Pearson learned his lesson about chasing varmints in the woods." The deeper voice chuckled.

"He has other lessons to learn," Abram said, his tone sharp and without the joviality of the other man's. "Tell him to leave me alone."

"I'll tell him," the man answered. "Although I doubt it'll do any good."

The voices became fainter, but even though the danger subsided, Miriam continued to tremble. Serpent had been too close.

Abram would come to get her, she felt sure, when the men had left the area. She and Abram would return to the farmhouse where she would remain until the roadblock was lifted.

But would Serpent continue to search for her? And if he found her, what would happen then?

SIX

The next morning Miriam stood at the kitchen window and peered at the mountain road, searching for any sign of a dark sedan. Yesterday Abram had returned to the woods and found her as soon as the two lawmen had left the area. Grateful though she was, Miriam was still concerned about her safety.

She had risen early to help Abram's sister. Apples needed to be peeled and pies baked for market, but the nervous churning in her stomach made her want to hide upstairs, away from the peering eyes of anyone who might pass by the farm.

Emma seemed oblivious to Miriam's anxiety and chatted amicably as she worked. Stepping away from the window, Miriam wrapped her arms around her waist, debating how to still her unease.

"As I mentioned last night, I have many pies to bake," Emma said as she placed a bowlful of apples on the table. "You will help me?"

Longing to allay the tension that tightened her shoulders, Miriam reached for the apple peeler. Using her hands would be therapeutic and might take her mind off the man who wanted to do her harm. Plus, Emma and Abram had provided her safe lodging. The least she could do was to help with the baking.

After peeling more than a dozen apples, Miriam heard Abram outside and, stepping to the sink for a drink of water, she peered from the window. "Does your brother ever stop working?"

Emma scooped flour into her cupped hand and then dropped it into the mixing bowl. "A farm requires work. He has a shop in addition. Livestock to care for, crops to grow."

"And you make pies to sell at market," Miriam said as she placed the now empty water glass next to the sink.

"Our apples are plentiful and the *Englisch* enjoy my baked goods. It lets me help Abram with the expenses."

"You help him with many things, Emma."

She smiled meekly. "We work together. He needs someone to cook his meals and wash his clothes. To put up the vegetables from the garden."

"The jobs his wife did."

"That is right. Without a wife, he could not handle the farm in addition to the house. Plus, it brings comfort knowing that I am helping offset some of the expenses by selling my pies at market. Work is not a bad thing."

"No. Of course not. And you're a good sister to care for him, yet surely you want a husband and a home of your own."

"*Gott* will provide when the time is right."

"You mean when Abram has found a wife."

Emma nodded sheepishly. "The problem is that he does not seem interested."

"Are you perhaps too accommodating?"

Emma glanced at Miriam. "What are you saying?"

"Abram doesn't look for another wife because you take care of him."

The Amish woman blushed. "I do not think that is the case. He would take a wife for more reasons than to share the work."

Miriam had to smile. "Is there no Amish man who strikes your fancy?"

"Most of those who are looking for a wife are younger."

"I can't believe Abram is the only widower in your community."

"Actually, Isaac Beiler lives nearby. He owns a dairy. You can see his farm from the front windows. He has one son. A sweet boy named Daniel."

Miriam returned to the table and continued peeling apples. Emma made the piecrust and rolled it into perfect circles that fit the disposable pie pans.

The women sliced the apples and added sugar, cinnamon, nutmeg and a pinch of salt before they filled the shells and covered the tart fruit with a latticed top crust.

"You baked at home?" Emma asked, watching as Miriam fluted the edges of the shells.

"My mother never baked, but I always enjoyed working in the kitchen."

Emma nodded with approval. "You seem to know what you are doing."

Later, when Emma pulled the last of the pies from the oven, Miriam inhaled the savory aroma that permeated the kitchen with a welcoming warmth of home and hearth, what Miriam had always longed for in her own house. Regrettably her mother's sharp rhetoric, especially as the dementia changed her personality, had dispelled any feelings of welcome or warmth.

Once she and Emma had cleaned the kitchen, the Amish woman pulled a bowl from the cupboard. "I will start cooking for the evening meal."

Miriam glanced at the cupboard, surprised by what she saw laying on top. "Is that a rifle?"

"*Yah*. Abram hunts. Sometimes I go with him."

"I wouldn't think—"

Emma tilted her head. "We hunt for food, Miriam. Deer, rabbits, wild turkeys."

"Is the gun loaded?" Miriam asked.

"What good would it be if it were not? Foxes and coyotes come after the livestock. We must keep them safe."

Miriam nodded. "From what I've seen, Emma, you work as hard as your brother."

Emma winked. "Some say the women work harder. We are up early to light the stove in the morning and the last to hug the children at night."

A knock at the door startled both of them.

"Check first to see who's there," Miriam warned. Her pulse pounded with dread. What if Serpent had returned?

Emma peered from the window and then rose on tiptoe to look down upon the person, evidently a very little person, standing on the back porch.

Emma laughed. "It is Daniel." She opened the door wide. "Let me help you with the milk."

An adorable boy, not more than five or six, stepped into the kitchen. He carried two large glass jugs that he placed on the floor just inside the door.

"Daniel is our milk delivery man. He lives on the farm just across the way."

The dairy run by the widower. Miriam stepped closer, totally taken with the boy's sparkling blue eyes and bowl-cut blond hair. His rosy cheeks and cautious smile instantly stole her heart.

"Daniel brings us milk from his father's dairy," Emma explained.

"You must be very strong," Miriam enthused, "to carry such heavy jugs so far."

The boy's chest puffed out and he nodded as if knowing the delivery job demanded not only brawn but also expertise and skill.

"Daniel, you have come at the perfect time." Emma pointed to the pies cooling on the sideboard. "Perhaps you would like a slice before you return home."

"*Yah*, I would like that. *Danki*."

The boy took a seat at the table and eagerly attacked the pie Emma placed in front of him. Miriam poured a glass of milk for the young lad and, before he lifted the glass to his lips, the door opened. Abram stepped inside, bringing with him the smell of fresh straw and lumber and the outdoors.

He smiled seeing their guest. "Daniel, did you save some pie for me?"

"*Yah*. Miriam will pour you a glass of milk, too."

She quickly cut a slice for Abram while he washed his hands and face. He returned to the kitchen with his hair neatly combed and his angular face scrubbed clean and ruddy from labor, and sat across from the boy. "I saw you helping your *datt* in the field. You did a fine job with the horses."

The boy beamed as he shoved another forkful of pie into his mouth. "I am a hard worker."

"I know you are. Your father relies on your help."

"He says we need a woman to help, too."

Miriam couldn't help but notice Emma's reaction. The color rose in her cheeks as she returned the cut pie to the sideboard.

"Your father would make some woman a good husband," Abram added, seemingly oblivious to his sister's reaction.

"He says I need a mother," the boy added without hesitation.

"And what do you say, Daniel?" Abram pressed.

"I say *Gott* will provide."

Abram chuckled. "You have a good head on your shoulders. Perhaps you need a bit more pie."

"*Datt* waits for me. I must go." He cleared his plate and fork from the table and handed them to Emma. "*Danki*."

She quickly wrapped a whole pie in a strip of cheese-cloth and tied it with a knot. "Here, Daniel. Take this home for you and your father."

The boy's eyes widened.

"Carry it with two hands," she instructed, pointing him toward the door. "I will watch you from the porch."

The boy's expression clouded. "But you never watch me."

She glanced at Abram. "Today I will."

No doubt, Emma sensed Abram's unease. Once Daniel said goodbye and he and Emma left the house, Miriam rinsed the dishes in the sink.

"You have done a good job with the baking," Abram said, eyeing the rows of pies cooling on the sideboard.

She was surprised by his statement. "How do you know I was involved?"

He rose and carried his plate and fork to the sink.

"Because your face is streaked with flour." He wiped his hands on a nearby towel and dropped the cloth onto the counter.

Turning, he gently flicked white powder from her cheek. His touch was light and brief, and her skin drank in his nearness as if she were desperate for some sign of acceptance. She leaned closer, inhaling the clean scent on a man who enjoyed nature and the outdoors.

Emma's voice could be heard calling goodbye to Daniel, but all Miriam thought about was Abram's touch and the beat of his heart when she had rested her head on his chest yesterday.

His fingers dropped to her lips. "It looks like a bit of sugary apple caught at the side of your mouth. That's how I could tell you were hard at work. The pie I tasted was delicious, so I thank you for preparing it for me."

"I... I..."

She could hardly think of anything to say. Her mind

kept remembering when she had been wrapped in his arms and wished to be there once again. Then she wouldn't have to worry about what had happened on the mountain road and that a man with a vile tattoo was prowling the countryside looking for her.

Emma pushed open the kitchen door.

Abram stepped away, leaving Miriam overcome with a sense of loss.

He smiled at his sister and pointed to Miriam. "Rebecca's pies—" he started to say.

Miriam's breath caught. *Rebecca*? Abram had confused her for his wife. A pain stabbed her heart.

Why was she drawn to this man who was so totally different from her? A man who still loved a woman who had died some years earlier, a woman whose clothing Miriam was wearing?

Any interest Abram might have showed to her was really directed to his wife. He was confused by the dress. He wasn't touching Miriam's lips, he was yearning to touch his wife's.

"Excuse me." Miriam wiped her hands on the nearby towel. "I need to go to my room."

Seems Miriam had followed in her mother's footsteps. Her mother had trusted no one and wandered from town to town looking for acceptance that she'd never seemed to find. Her negative outlook on life had caused Miriam to keep a tight hold on her own heart, as well. She hadn't allowed anyone to come close, especially not a man who put her world into a spin.

"Are you all right?" Emma asked as she followed her up the stairs. "You appeared upset when Abram mentioned Rebecca's name. Her pies were never as golden brown as ours today, which was the point he was trying to make."

Miriam knew the truth. Abram had confused her for his wife.

"I'm tired, Emma. If you don't mind, I'd like to lie down for a bit."

"Yes, of course. You have been through so much."

After Abram's slip of the tongue, Miriam needed to make plans to leave Willkommen and head to Atlanta. But how would she contact Hannah? If they couldn't connect by phone, Miriam might be able to contact her via email. To do that, she would need a computer.

"You told me that the *Englisch* buy your baked goods," she said before Emma left the room.

The Amish woman nodded. "I have some regular customers who I count on weekly."

"Do any of them live nearby?"

"The Rogers's house is about four miles from here. They have a standing order of two loaves of bread, a pie and two dozen cookies each Saturday."

"Their house is situated along the road to Willkommen?"

"Actually, it sits back from the road. I used to take the route that crosses over the river. The bridge is not strong enough for an automobile, but a carriage can pass there. Although sometimes a horse can get spooked."

"That's the road that passes in front of your house?"

Emma nodded. "But Abram is worried about our safety, and he does not like the water."

"What do you mean?"

Emma shrugged. "I should not bring it up."

"But you mentioned it."

"I did, although I should not talk about Abram." She bit her lip and sighed. "His best friend when he was fourteen was an *Englischer*. Trevor was older and drove his father's car too fast. Abram was with him. There was a sharp curve and the car skidded off the road and into the lake."

Miriam could see the pain wash over Emma's face. "What happened to the *Englisch* boy?"

"Abram saved himself but—" Emma pulled in a stiff breath. "He could not save Trevor."

"I'm sorry, Emma."

"*Yah*, it was hard on all of us. Abram especially."

Miriam could only imagine how tragic the drowning had been.

"The accident happened in Tennessee, but the memory returns whenever Abram is around any body of water. For that reason, he stays away from the river and the bridge and, although a longer journey, we take the other fork in the road. While it causes us to backtrack, Abram does not have to worry about the bridge." Emma's face brightened. "I have an idea. You can go with me to the Rogers's house on Saturday. They are good people. You will like them."

"Do they have a computer?"

"I do not know about a computer, but I am sure they have a phone so you can call your sister."

By Saturday, Miriam hoped to be in Atlanta. She looked down at the blue dress she wore and brushed a smudge of white flour from the skirt. "I must wash my clothes, Emma. You need to show me where you placed them."

"I will wash next week. It is no trouble. Your things are in the barn, soaking since they were spotted with blood."

"You don't need to do my wash. Just tell me where you keep the soap or laundry detergent."

"You will see them near the wash barrel."

In addition to clean clothes, Miriam also needed money for her bus ticket. "I'll rest now and maybe go to the barn later," she said as a plan took hold.

"You will take the evening meal with us?"

"Yes, of course. I'll come downstairs later to help you prepare the food."

"Only if you feel strong enough. Perhaps I tired you too much with baking the pies."

"Absolutely not. I enjoyed the work."

"And I enjoyed the company."

Glancing out the window, Emma smiled. "I see Isaac is coming to visit."

Miriam stared over the Amish woman's shoulder and nudged Emma playfully. "He probably wants to thank you for the pie."

"Perhaps. Although I suspect he wants to talk to Abram. They are alike, those two, although in different ways."

Miriam raised her brow. "Meaning?"

"Isaac knows he must work within the Amish way, but he uses some other resources in his business." No doubt seeing Miriam's confusion, she added, "A dairy needs refrigeration if he is to sell to the *Englisch*."

"You mean Isaac uses electricity?"

"*Yah,* it is allowed, but the power runs only to the dairy barn. It is *verboten*—not allowed—in the house."

"The bishop sets the rules?" Miriam asked.

"We live by the *Ordnung*, but each bishop leads his own community. Some communities and some bishops are less strict in adhering to the old ways."

"Does Abram have electricity in his woodshop?"

Emma shook her head. "Abram would not, but he does use diesel fuel to run some of his woodworking machines. Diesel is allowed."

"I don't understand."

"Some members of our community came from Ethridge, Tennessee, years ago. You have heard of that town?"

Miriam nodded. "Abram mentioned it."

"Ethridge is made up mainly of Old Order Amish. They live as the Amish have since first coming to America. They do not have running water in their homes as we do here. Nor does anyone, even those doing business with the *Englisch*, use propane. Diesel motors are allowed, but that is all."

"Abram said part of the community left Ethridge and moved here."

Emma nodded. "A new community usually develops when a group of families have like ideas about the way they will live. Sometimes they move to find farmland, as Abram did."

"So your community is less conservative compared to Ethridge, where you grew up?"

"Except Abram. He remains very conservative."

"And his wife?" Miriam asked. "How did she feel?"

Emma smiled sweetly. "She loved Abram. What could she say?"

A knock sounded at the door below.

"It is Isaac." Emma tugged a strand of hair back from her face and hurried into the hallway. "I need to welcome him."

Emma's feelings for Isaac were obvious. Although Miriam had never loved a man, she had hoped to find someone someday. Someone who would walk through life at her side. Both of them in step and working together.

But love would have to wait. As much as she admired Abram and found his home and way of life peaceful, Miriam would never fit into the Amish community. Or could she?

Abram studied the wood he had stacked against the wall of his workshop. In times past, he had been considered a master craftsman. The work had brought joy and a steady income from the items he had sold in town. But that was before Rebecca had died.

He touched the arm of the hickory bentwood rocker he had only begun to make. For the last three years, it had remained a visible reminder of his deceased wife.

Deep in his heart, Abram knew Rebecca would have wanted him to find someone else. Emma had hinted at the fact several times. But he did not deserve happiness after what had happened. He had never verbalized his thoughts to his sister nor did he give voice to the question that troubled him now.

Why would he search for someone to replace Rebecca when his own stubbornness had claimed her life?

Yet ever since Miriam had appeared on his doorstep, he wondered if there could be something—or someone—else that would fill the void Rebecca's passing had left.

Abram shook his head with regret. He didn't need joy. He needed redemption. His father was right. He had been too easily taken off task as a youth. He would not let himself be thrown off course now.

The door to his shop opened and Isaac Beiler entered. Tall and stocky, the dairyman dipped his head in greeting. "Emma said I would find you here."

Abram left the rocker and stepped closer to his neighbor. "I thought you came for another pie." He was hard-pressed to stop the smile that tugged at his lips and he was glad when Isaac's eyes responded with twinkling good humor.

"Emma is always generous with her baked goods," Isaac said. "She is generous with her heart, as well. She invited Daniel and me to join you for supper this evening."

Isaac's wife had died thirteen months earlier. "Emma sees you losing weight, my friend. You and Daniel both need a good meal to fill your bellies. I do not know how you manage the dairy and the household. I would waste away if Emma were not living with me."

"She is a good woman." The neighbor rubbed his beard. "With Daniel, my thought was always to find a mother for my son."

"Yet in all these months, you have not found anyone?" Abram questioned what they both knew to be true.

Isaac sighed. "There is a woman, although I am not sure how she feels about me. With the dairy and raising my son, I have little time to court."

"Ah, but Isaac, you must make the time."

"By adding more hours to the day?" the neighbor smiled ruefully.

"There is always time for love."

"You are not one to follow your own advice, Abram."

The two men chuckled, but their joviality turned serious with Isaac's next comment.

"Daniel told me about the lady who has come into your home. I questioned Emma. She hesitated to tell me about the visitor until I mentioned seeing the sheriff's car on the road. She said the woman—Miriam—was injured and you gave her refuge. Your sister is worried about you, Abram."

"Worried? In what way?"

"That you do not realize what could come of this. Did you tell your uncle about the visitor?"

"I tried, but he needed to get back to town and did not have time to hear me out."

"What about the bishop? He has time to listen."

Abram did not want the bishop or any of the elders involved. The fewer people who knew about Miriam, the better. At least until Samuel returned to Willkommen.

"The bishop provides wise guidance," Abram explained. "But I do not need his counsel at this time."

He hoped Isaac would be satisfied with his answer, but the neighbor pushed on.

"Deputy Idler stopped by the dairy yesterday and told me about the abandoned car and the older woman's body found in the trunk. The timing makes me think your houseguest is somehow involved. Have you questioned her?"

Although Abram would rather not discuss the newcomer, he knew Isaac could be trusted.

"A man held her captive. He is on the loose. When Samuel returns to Willkommen Miriam will tell him what happened. Until then, she must remain hidden, and the best place to do that is here with me."

"She wears Amish clothing."

"Because she has nothing else to wear. The bishop would not want her going without clothing."

Isaac shrugged. "He would not."

"Once Samuel returns, the problem will be resolved. You understand I am acting out of concern for the woman. She was hurt and injured. I had to take her in. Is Emma unsettled by her presence?"

"She likes Miriam, but as I mentioned, she is worried about you."

"Emma worries too much. I am fine, Isaac."

"And what happens if the man who held her captive comes after you or after Emma? I do not need to remind you, Abram. The Amish way is one of peace, not conflict."

"If a fox is killing chickens in your coup, Isaac, do you stand by and watch? Or do you go after the fox?"

Isaac lowered his gaze and kicked at a mound of sawdust on the floor. "Be careful, my friend."

"We will be fine."

Glancing up, Isaac nodded. "Then I will return home now. Daniel and I will see you this evening."

After his neighbor left, Abram continued to think about Isaac's comments.

Was Abram making good choices concerning Miriam? He wanted to keep her safe. Hiding her on his farm was the right decision, but Emma was worried. Was she worried about their safety or Abram's heart?

SEVEN

Peering from her bedroom window, Miriam spied the Amish neighbor leaving Abram's workshop. He joined Emma at the front of the house where she was talking to Daniel. The young boy played with a stick that he threw in the air and then ran to catch. Bear sauntered around the corner of the house as if wanting to join the fun.

Even from her lofty vantage point, Miriam noticed the warmth in Emma's expression as she laughed with the child. Hopefully, the dairy farmer and his son would continue to occupy Emma's attention for some time.

Miriam turned her gaze to the workshop. From what she knew of Abram's routine, he would hopefully stay put for at least an hour or two.

With no time to lose, Miriam hurried down the stairway and out the kitchen door. She wrapped the black cape around her shoulders and raced along the path she and Abram had walked her first morning on the farm.

Miriam's car had bogged down near the river just past the edge of Abram's property. Surely the police had finished their search and, unless they had hauled the vehicle off to Petersville, she expected to find her car exactly where she had left it.

Thoughts of her mother's body found in the trunk made

her sick with grief. She fisted her hands and forced the thoughts to flee. She couldn't mourn her mother now. She had to think of finding her sister, Sarah, and getting to Atlanta.

Still hoping to find her cell, Miriam kept her gaze on the edges of the path she walked and only occasionally glanced over her shoulder to make certain no one was following her. She didn't want Abram to stop her.

She needed to leave the area and that required a bus ticket, which meant she had to retrieve the emergency stash of money from her car. The police would have searched her vehicle but, how thoroughly, she wasn't sure. Even if they had looked at the maintenance manual in her glove compartment, hopefully they hadn't riffled through the pages.

A stiff wind blew across the pasture. She pulled the cape more tightly around her shoulders and increased her pace. She didn't have time to dawdle. Miriam had to retrieve the money from her car and return to the farmhouse before Abram or Emma noticed her absence.

All the while she walked, she listened for the sound of a car engine, knowing she would have to hide if she saw Serpent's dark sedan driving along the mountain road. To her relief, all she heard was the caw of crows flying overhead.

Nearing the fence that edged Abram's property, Miriam hurried forward to the open gate through which she must have passed the night of her escape. Leaving the pasture, she looked back at the farmhouse still visible in the distance. Once again she thought of the light shining in the window that had been her beacon of hope when she was trying to elude Serpent.

Turning her back on the peaceful scene, Miriam scurried deeper into the underbrush where the thick growth of pine trees mixed with hardwoods blocked the sunlight.

The temperature dropped and the sharp bramble forced her to slow her pace.

Carefully she picked her way around the prickly bushes that caught at her dress. Two nights earlier, she hadn't worried about thorns or sharp branches. She'd only thought of staying alive.

Skirting a particularly large bush, she inadvertently stepped on a twig that broke underfoot with a loud *crack*. The sound seemed amplified in the dense forest. She stopped behind a gathering of bushes to catch her breath and listen. Surely no one was close by, but she had to be careful.

As much as she wanted to keep moving forward, an internal, niggling voice cautioned her to bide her time. The forest stilled but another sound filled her ears. Rushing water.

Peering through the underbrush, she spied the river. The moving water was what she had heard while being held in the cabin and brought back memories of the hateful man who had held her captive.

She blinked her eyes, trying to clear the vision that sickened her. Serpent.

Was he real or imagined?

She blinked again but the vision remained.

Her heart stopped. The man who had held her captive stood staring in her direction.

Miriam's pulse raced. He must have heard the twig break. Although the thicket behind which she hid offered protection, she knew any additional movement would have him running to investigate.

He pursed his lips, took a step forward and stopped.

Please, God, don't let him see me.

Serpent stood still for a long moment and then turned toward her vehicle.

Sending up a prayer of thanks, Miriam watched him wrap a handkerchief around his hand, open the driver's door and peer inside. Bending down, he felt under the seat before he rounded the car, opened the passenger door and rummaged through the glove compartment.

Leaves rustled behind her. Startled, she glanced over her shoulder. A squirrel scurried through the underbrush. Letting out a tiny sigh of relief, she turned her gaze back to the river's edge.

Serpent had disappeared.

Her heart crashed against her chest. A lump of fear lodged in her throat. Frantically she flicked her gaze around the clearing and then back to the car. Where had he gone?

Another swish of movement sounded behind her.

She started to turn.

A hand clamped over her mouth.

Powerful arms grabbed her and held her tightly against a rock-hard chest.

She gasped, fearing her fate. Serpent had captured her again.

Abram's heart beat out of his chest from fear so strong it had taken his breath away. He had seen Serpent. The man who had hurt Miriam. She had come so close to stepping into the open and startling the horrific man from his search.

A few minutes ago Abram had peered through the window of his woodshop and had seen her scurrying through the pasture after Isaac had left him. Following after her, Abram had spotted the man with the tattoo and feared Miriam was unaware of the hated man's presence. Thankfully, Abram had gotten to Miriam before Serpent had spotted her.

"Serpent is prowling in the bushes," he whispered in her ear as he held her close to his heart. "If you move, he will hear you."

She must have recognized his voice because she stopped struggling and relaxed against his chest. Turning her head ever so slightly placed her lips close to Abram's. Too close.

His heart jerked from her nearness.

"Where did he go?" she asked, her voice shaky with fear.

"I do not know."

"But you saw him, Abram. Right?"

He nodded. "*Yah*, I did."

"You saw the scarf around his neck. He's trying to hide the serpent tattoo, but it's there. He's the same man who chased after me in the woods."

"And the one who held you captive." Anger welled up within Abram directed toward the man who had accosted Miriam.

"Stay here," he cautioned. "I will circle the clearing and try to determine whether Serpent is still in the area."

Miriam grabbed his hand tightly. "Be careful. He's evil."

"Do not fear for my safety." Abram had to warn her. "But if he finds you, scream. I will hear you."

She nodded, her face void of color and her eyes wide with fear.

Abram stepped away from her. His whole being wanted to keep her close, but he needed to determine where Serpent had gone.

His hunting skills proved useful as he made his way stealthily through the underbrush. Nearing a break in the tree line, he had a clear view of the mountain road.

A dark sedan sat parked on the side of the pavement.

Serpent stood nearby, staring at smoke rising from a chimney visible through the trees.

Old Man Jacobs's cabin.

From that location Ezra Jacobs had a view of the road as it curved around the mountain. As Samuel had mentioned, Ezra had seen the cars racing along the roadway two nights ago and had called the sheriff. What else had he seen?

As Abram watched, Serpent opened the driver's door and slipped in behind the wheel. Making a sharp U-turn he gunned the engine and drove up the mountain on the road that led to Petersville. Was he going back to town or back to the cabin where he had held Miriam? If only Abram could follow him to find the hiding spot.

But Miriam was waiting for him. He needed to take her home and lock the doors behind them. Then Abram would pay a visit to Old Man Jacobs. He wanted to find out what the man had seen. Two cars driving much too fast down the mountain, or had he seen even more than that?

When Abram stepped back to the clearing, he saw Miriam in her car rummaging through the glove compartment.

"I told you to remain hidden," he said as he neared.

"I saw Serpent drive away. I needed my cell phone charger." She held it up along with a wad of bills. "And some money I kept in the glove compartment. I'm glad the police didn't find the bills or haul my car away."

"The Petersville police department has had problems in the past. This time their oversight worked to your advantage. What about your cell phone?"

"It's not here, but with the charger, I'll be able to use the phone when I do find it."

"I have money, Miriam. You could have asked me if you needed anything."

"You've already done too much."

Abram pointed to the smoke visible through the tree

line in the distance. "An old man lives in a cabin there where the smoke is rising. I want to talk to him. He may have seen something."

"I'll go with you."

"It would not be wise."

"I'm concerned about my own safety, but I'm even more worried about Sarah. The man might know something about my sister. Or he may know about the cabin where we both were held. Let's go now," Miriam suggested.

"The distance is farther than it looks. I will take the buggy."

Miriam was silent as they walked back to the house. Hopefully she realized she would be safer remaining at the farm. But from what he knew about Miriam, once she got an idea in her head, there was no changing her mind.

Abram was not used to headstrong women or *Englisch* women who spoke their mind. He almost chuckled. In a way, he found it refreshing, which is something he would not share with the bishop or even Isaac Beiler.

Some things were better left unsaid.

EIGHT

"I'm going with you," Miriam said as Abram hitched Nellie to the buggy.

"You are staying here with Emma."

She shook her head. "I'm accompanying you."

"Serpent may be in the area," Abram said, no doubt trying to convince her of the folly of riding with him.

She looked down at the blue dress and apron. "He won't recognize me in Amish clothing, Abram. You needn't fear."

He dipped his head in agreement. "As you said, he should not recognize you wearing the *plain* clothing, unless he catches sight of your pretty face. I do not want to chance putting you in danger."

Bear trotted forward and nuzzled her leg. Miriam patted the dog's head then, gripping the side of the buggy, she hefted herself into the rig.

"You don't understand, Abram." She settled onto the rear seat. "I can't stay here at the house while you talk to a man who might know something about my sister. I'm going with you. You don't have a choice."

Abram muttered something that sounded like German under his breath, followed by, "Amish women are not so brazen."

She had to fight to keep from smiling. "You find me brazen?"

He shrugged. "Would 'determined' be a better choice of word?"

"Brazen or determined. Either one suits me just fine. I don't want to stay at the farm and wonder what you've found out from Mr. Jacobs. I need to see the area where he lives. I've forgotten much of what happened when I was held captive. No telling what might trigger my memory."

She nodded her head decidedly. "I heard running water, like the sound of the river scurrying past the cabin where I was held. If we find the cabin, I may remember who shot my mother. It wasn't Serpent. From the little I recall, the other man seemed in charge, as if Serpent could have been working for him. I need to find that man and also the red-headed guy who hauled Sarah away."

"It is my desire to find those men as well, but I still want you to stay here." Abram shrugged his shoulders as if wondering how he could convince her otherwise. "My uncle will bring everyone involved to justice, you can be sure of that."

"Your uncle's out of town, Abram, and I refuse to wait. We'll go together to Old Man Jacobs. We'll explore the back mountain roads. Something might come to light."

Once Nellie was hitched, he climbed into the buggy and sat on the first seat directly in front of Miriam.

Emma stepped onto the back porch. "I am worried about both of you."

"You are too much filled with concern, my sister."

But she had every right to be upset. A stranger had burst into their peaceful lives and thrown them into havoc.

"We won't be gone long." Miriam tried to sound optimistic as she waved goodbye.

Abram jostled the reins and Nellie started forward, the buggy swaying side to side in a comfortable rhythm Miriam found soothing.

With another flick of the reins, the mare increased her pace just after they turned onto the mountain road. The wind buffered Miriam's face, the morning air brisk and fresh. She settled back in the seat.

"There are blankets in the rear if you are cold," Abram shared. "You can reach them, *yah*?"

She turned, grabbed the woolen throws and wrapped one around her legs. She placed the second one over Abram's legs.

He smiled but kept his eyes on the road. "The morning is cool but not cold. I am fine, Miriam Miller."

Yet he didn't remove the throw.

The ride up the mountain took less time than Miriam had imagined. Abram pulled up on the reins and encouraged Nellie onto a narrow dirt path that angled more sharply up the mountain. The path was pitted with holes that caused the buggy to sway wildly back and forth.

Abram groaned. "We will stop here," he said when they came to a small clearing. "And walk the rest of the way."

He helped her out of the buggy, his hands strong around her waist. Once on the ground, she looked up, realizing how tall he really was.

Standing so close to Abram made her breath catch. He stared down at her with questioning eyes that made her heart pound. Was it his wife he saw when he looked at her? The thought made Miriam step back, but the buggy prevented her from going far.

Abram swallowed hard and dropped his hold on her. "Ezra Jacobs's cabin is nearby."

She glanced at the underbrush, the steep incline and the dirt path pocked with holes. "He could use a bit of home improvement."

"A recluse does not wish for company."

They started up the hill together. Abram reached for her arm and guided her along the path.

Her first inclination was to refuse his help, but the sincerity of his gaze made her realize she didn't need to prove her independence with Abram.

Having a man at her side was a pleasant change. She enjoyed the strength of his hand and the gentleness of his hold.

Once at the top of the steep incline they stepped into a larger clearing. A cabin sat nestled in the trees, overrun with vines. The porch listed and the stairs looked far too rickety for Abram's large frame, but he climbed the steps and knocked forcefully on the door.

When no one answered, he reached for the knob and pushed the door open. Miriam peered around him into the dark interior.

Although small, the cabin was neat and tidy. The floor was swept and the narrow bed pushed against the far wall was covered with a colorful blanket. An old beagle with graying hair lay curled on a small rug at the foot of the bed.

The dog raised his head, wagged his tail and hobbled toward them. Miriam bent to pat him then, seeing the blanket move, she grabbed Abram's arm and pointed to the cot.

Together they entered the cabin and approached the bed. Her heart stopped as she leaned closer to Abram. "Is he all right?"

Abram touched the man's arm. "Ezra, it is Abram Zook. You need to awake."

The old man's eyes fluttered open. He stared up at Abram then furrowed his brow. His voice was crusty with sleep when he spoke. "You're trespassing."

Abram smiled. "Perhaps, but I thought you were dead."

Just that fast, the man pushed aside the blanket, rolled to his side and sat up, wiping his eyes. "Tarnation, Abram.

I'm breathing, ain't I? Don't know why you came barging into my cabin unannounced. A simple knock at the door would have raised me from my sleep."

The beagle stood next to the bed and waited expectantly until the old man scratched behind the dog's ears.

Relieved that Ezra appeared fit, Miriam stepped closer. "Sir, I'm Miriam Miller. Can we get you something? Maybe a glass of water?"

"Coffee. Strong and hot. The pot's on the counter ready to go. Just hit the button. Pull three cups from the cabinet and you can join me."

His gaze narrowed. "You said you're a Miller. Any kin to Harold Miller in Petersville?"

"I'm not sure. Does he have daughters named Leah or Annie?"

"Harold's got six sons. No daughters. His wife died when the last one was born."

"I'm sorry."

"We all were." He pointed to the kitchen area. "Turn that switch on the coffeepot, hear? A man could die of thirst, waiting for a cup of coffee, as slow as you're moving."

Miriam chuckled under her breath and hurried to do the man's bidding.

Abram patted the older man's shoulder. "Ezra, I talked to Sheriff Kurtz yesterday. He said you saw two cars racing down the mountain road the other night."

The old man nodded. "One had flashing lights."

"Did you think it was a sheriff's car?" Abram asked.

"Could have been, or one of those cop cars from Petersville. They patrol the road up to Pine Lodge Mountain."

"It runs by your cabin?"

"That's right. On a quiet night, I can hear cars driving to the lodge."

"Sheriff Kurtz wondered if you could provide more information about what you saw."

"You mean the ruckus in the woods?"

Abram leaned closer. "Tell me what happened."

Jacobs shrugged and rubbed his brow. "Wish I could, but my mind plays tricks on me. I remember some things and forget others. Couldn't remember much yesterday when I talked to the deputies. 'Spect I won't be able to remember any more today."

"Let's go back to what you do remember," Miriam said as she returned to his bedside. "Have you seen me before?"

Ezra stared up at her and then shook his head. "Seems I'd remember you."

"Why's that?"

"You look like someone I used to know."

"Leah Miller was my mother? Did you know her?"

"Can't recall. Names don't stay. Only thing that seems to stick are faces. I've seen you or seen someone who looked like you, but I can't tell you where."

"Is there another cabin nearby?" she asked. "Or did you see me with a man who had a snake tattooed on his neck?"

Ezra shook his head. "Can't recall."

"What about a pretty blond girl?"

He rubbed his jaw. "I haven't seen anyone with blond hair for a while."

"Does that mean you haven't seen a blond-haired woman in the area?"

He nodded. "'Spect that's what it means."

Miriam sighed and turned to stare at the light coming through the still open doorway. Her gaze shifted to the cell phone on a nearby side table. The phone was a basic model without text or internet capability.

"Is that your cell, Mr. Jacobs?" she asked.

"Sure 'nough. You need to make a call?"

"If you wouldn't mind? I'd like to contact my sister in Atlanta."

"Won't be a problem. Long distance don't cost any extra, but go outside. You can't pick up anything in here."

Ezra's lips quivered into a half smile. "'Course, most times I can't get the right number plugged in with those small buttons." He pointed to a pair of reading glasses. "Helps if I use the spectacles. You need them?"

She shook her head. "Not the glasses, but I appreciate you letting me use the phone."

"What about the coffee?" he asked as she headed for the door.

"It's brewing."

Miriam hurried onto the porch and called directory assistance in Atlanta. Once connected to the automated operator, she requested the phone number for Hannah Miller and then repeated the name twice for clarity. Making herself understood was a challenge, but she responded to the prompts as best she could and was crestfallen when the search failed.

Miriam disconnected, feeling a heaviness to her heart. If only she could talk to Hannah.

She stepped back into the cabin, laid the phone on the counter and inhaled the rich aroma of fresh-brewed coffee.

"Did you contact your sister?" Abram asked.

Miriam shook her head. "Evidently, Hannah doesn't have a landline."

She moved into the makeshift kitchen. "What do you take in your coffee, Mr. Jacobs?"

"You're making me feel old. My name's Ezra and I take my coffee black."

She quickly fixed his coffee and placed it on his bedside table, then poured a cup for Abram and one for herself.

The hearty roast was hot and good. Even Ezra seemed

to rally after his first sip. "I always drink my coffee at the table," he said as if she should have realized his cup needed to be placed there.

He gripped the metal-frame headboard and pulled himself to his feet. The beagle stood next to him, and Abram hovered close by, ready to offer a hand. Ezra walked slowly, but without problem, to the table. With a huff, he pulled out a chair and sat with a sigh of relief. The dog dropped to the floor at his side.

Miriam selected a chair across the table and Abram slipped into a seat on the opposite end. Once they were situated, he looked at the old man and smiled. "Tell us what you *do* remember, Ezra."

"Just the two cars racing along the roadway. I had fallen asleep sitting in the rocker by the fireplace."

He looked down at the faithful mutt who wagged his tail as if begging for a treat.

"Gus woke me." Ezra scratched the dog's ears. "He needed to do his business. When I opened the door to let him out, I heard the squeal of tires and the sound of an engine. Peered through the trees. Didn't see much except the flashing light."

"Have you noticed anyone walking through your property recently?"

The old man's eyes widened. "I told you about the sheriff's deputy."

Abram smiled. "You did tell us. Have you seen anyone else?"

Ezra closed his eyes for a long moment. Miriam wasn't sure if he was thinking or if he had fallen back to sleep.

"I've got a face." He blinked his lids open, a look of pride in his rheumy eyes.

"Someone you've seen recently?" Miriam pressed.

"That's right."

"Is it someone from around here?"

"Can't say where he's from. All I've got is his face. He's skinny as a beanpole with sunken cheeks that make his eyes kind of bug out."

Miriam's heart fluttered. She leaned across the table and stared at Ezra. "You saw a thin man nearby?"

"Tall and thin, although I can't remember exactly where I saw him."

Her pulse raced. "Was there anything else about the man that stands out in your mind?"

Ezra nodded and pointed to the top of his head. "His hair."

Miriam glanced at Abram, who was staring at her, his face tense.

"What was it about his hair?" she asked, knowing before Ezra said anything else.

"His hair was kind of wiry and puffed out around his pale face. But it was the color that I remember." Ezra dropped his hand back to Gus's neck. "The guy had bright red hair."

A red-haired man, tall and skinny. The man she had seen at Serpent's cabin. The man who had taken Sarah.

"Was a woman with him?"

Again the old man closed his eyes. Miriam counted off the seconds, but when he opened his eyes, he shook his head. "I don't remember any other faces."

"A young woman, blond hair, blue eyes," she prompted, hoping to prod his recall.

Again he shook his head.

Miriam's heart shattered. The red-haired man had been spotted, but Ezra hadn't seen her sister. If only he could remember something more.

She glanced at Abram, hoping he could help, but all she

saw was sorrow in his expression, as if he knew the questions that tugged at her heart.

What had happened to her sister?

And was Sarah alive…or dead?

Seeing the pain on Miriam's face, Abram wanted to reach out and take her hand. The expectation in her eyes when the old man had mentioned the redhead had been dashed when Ezra failed to remember her sister.

Abram would never share his concern with Miriam, but he feared for Sarah's safety—if she was still alive.

Had there been other women taken on the mountain? Travelers driving over the narrow roads, unsure of the terrain? Women were vulnerable and especially so at night.

Abram's stomach soured, thinking of how women would be used. *Gott* have mercy on Sarah and on any other women caught in such a wicked net of perversion.

He and Miriam needed information about Serpent. They also needed to find the ring leader who had killed Miriam's mother as well as the red-haired man who had Sarah.

"Ezra, keep thinking back over the last few days and try to remember what you may have seen. Miriam and I will visit you again."

The old man reached down to pat his dog. "'Spect Gus and I will be here when you return."

"Is there anything you need?" Miriam stood and glanced into the small kitchen. "Food or household items?"

"Don't need a thing. My boy lives in Chattanooga. He comes down to visit at times and keeps me well stocked. You don't need to worry about me."

But Abram was worried. Something sinister was happening on the mountain.

Concerned for Miriam's safety, Abram checked outside before he hurried her back to the buggy. Once she was settled in the rear seat, he flicked the reins for Nellie to begin the journey home.

Leaving Ezra's property, they bumped their way down the potholed path and turned left onto the mountain road. Nellie picked up her speed once she turned onto the pavement, as if knowing they were headed home.

Nearing the next bend in the road the sound of a car alerted them to oncoming traffic. Abram eased up on the reins as a car zipped around the turn.

A black sedan with a stocky man at the wheel. He barely glanced at Abram before he accelerated and the car sped up the hill.

Miriam gasped. Abram glanced back, seeing the color drain from her face.

"It was him." She groaned. "Serpent."

Abram peered around the corner of the buggy, but the car had disappeared around the bend.

She grasped Abram's arm. "Did he see me?"

Abram shook his head, wanting to reassure her. "He was looking at the mountain, Miriam. He did not notice either of us."

At least, that was Abram's hope.

NINE

Abram was on edge the rest of the afternoon after seeing Serpent. Even while grooming the horses and handling the afternoon chores, he kept watch over the house in case the kidnapper came searching for Miriam.

He had cautioned her to remain indoors, away from the windows, and to hurry upstairs if anyone knocked at the door. The house would provide protection. At least, that was his hope.

By evening some of his anxiety had eased and he looked forward to seeing Isaac again, and especially Daniel. The young boy brought joy to his heart with his innocence and wonder.

For too long, caring for his farm had sapped the life from Abram. When had he changed? he wondered, thinking back to when life was good. Easy enough to realize. The joy had left the night Rebecca died.

The weight of his grief had been too much to bear at first. Each night he had reached for Rebecca in his bed, only to find nothing; even the sweet smell of her had disappeared all too soon. Some days he couldn't remember her face, which caused him pain.

After finishing his work, Abram washed his hands at the pump outside. He shook off the water and dried them on a towel that hung nearby.

Daniel stepped onto the porch and waved a greeting. "Emma said to tell you that the food will be ready to eat in half an hour's time."

"That is good. I am hungry." He smiled at the boy. "I am sure you are, too."

"*Datt* says I am always hungry." His blue eyes were wide with innocence.

Abram's heart tugged, thinking of the son he and Rebecca had been expecting. A child who had died in delivery due to Abram's stubbornness and failure to listen to his wife.

Suddenly, Abram was no longer hungry.

"Tell Emma I must go to the barn first."

"I will tell her." The boy scurried into the kitchen.

A chill blew off the mountain and pulled at Abram's shirt. He hurried to the barn, needing time to collect himself before he sat at table.

Bear greeted him but he ignored the dog, passed the horses' stalls and headed to a storage room. Opening the door, he pulled back a tarp and stood staring at the cradle he had made for his child. The hardwood gleamed with oil he had painstakingly rubbed into the cherry wood. Each spindle had been sanded with love for the child he never knew.

He let out a deep sigh, wishing he could in some way go back and start his life again. Then he realized the foolishness of his thoughts. Mistakes once made could never be unmade; a truth he had learned the hard way as a youth. Emma still bore the marks of his mistake. Trevor's death was all too poignant of a reminder, as well.

"It's beautiful."

He turned to find Miriam staring through the doorway. Bear sat at her feet.

"Did you make the cradle?" she asked.

"Yah." Turning from her tender gaze, he replaced the tarp, stepped from the small storage room and closed the door behind him.

"Your workmanship is lovely, Abram. Do you sell your cradles at the market?"

"I have only made one cradle."

She nodded as if filling in the portion he did not wish to tell her. "I'm sorry about your baby."

"It was *Gott*'s will." Brought on by Abram's stubborn pride to live the Rule as he felt his ancestors had done with no deviation. If only he had listened to his wife. Rebecca had said he was unbending because of the mistakes he had made in his youth and his desire to prove himself to his father. Perhaps she had been right.

"Emma sent you to find me?" he asked.

Miriam shook her head. "She and Isaac are talking. Supper won't be ready for a while. I'm looking for my clothes. Emma said they're soaking in a bucket."

He pointed to the opening at the rear of the barn. "You will find the wash bucket through there."

When she started for the doorway, he touched her arm.

"You do not need to be concerned about your clothing. Emma washes at the first of the week."

"The last thing Emma needs is more work. I'm perfectly capable of doing laundry."

"By hand?"

She nodded. "Of course. Do you think I'm some type of prima donna who shies away from work?"

He shook his head. "No, you are industrious and determined."

She stopped and looked up. He could see the flecks of gold in her brown eyes.

His heart raced and a tightness pulled at his gut. How could he react so strongly to her nearness when seconds earlier he had been grieving for his wife? He did not understand his response to this woman who had made his life seem inside out and upside down.

"You surprise me, Miriam Miller."

She raised a brow. "Because?"

"Because I do not understand the *Englisch* ways. What is it you need?" he asked, recognizing the deeper meaning of his question. What did this *Englisch* woman need or want with an Amish man who lived a *plain* life?

"I need to go to Willkommen."

"Quigley told me the roadblock will not be lifted until tomorrow night. The following is market day. We will go to Willkommen then."

"I'd like to go sooner than that so I can contact Hannah."

"You have remembered your sister's cell phone number?"

Miriam shook her head. "No, but I can email her."

Even if the roadblock ended, going to Willkommen would be dangerous. Did she not remember Serpent passing them on the mountain road?

"Day after tomorrow will be soon enough," he stated.

"Emma mentioned *Englisch* neighbors that might have a computer."

Abram raised his hand as if to cut her off.

She sighed with frustration then turned and hurried out the door at the back of the barn. Bear scurried after her.

Abram wanted to grab her hand and tell her he would take her to town this instant if that was what she wanted, but making such a dangerous trip would mean he was losing his mind as well as his heart.

Miriam had trouble eating her supper. The food was delicious, but the man sitting across the table from her was the problem. At least Emma and Isaac were having a nice time. From the flow of chatter, they didn't seem to notice Miriam's silence. Daniel sat next to her, equally quiet, although he kept glancing at her plate.

"You do not like the food?" he whispered, sounding much more grown up than his years.

She smiled, grateful for his thoughtfulness and relieved to have someone other than Abram on whom to focus.

"I nibbled on pie earlier and spoiled my appetite," she explained, hoping to deflect his concern.

"I had a big slice of pie, but I am still hungry."

"Growing boys need food."

He nodded in agreement and then turned back to his plate.

"Do you want more potatoes, Daniel?" Emma asked.

"*Yah*, please. And a biscuit."

"Son, you must wait until Emma asks," his father quickly reproved.

"But she asked if I wanted potatoes." The boy didn't see the problem, which brought a smile to Miriam's lips.

Forgetting herself, she glanced at Abram. Often pensive and solemn, tonight his eyes were bright. A smile curved his lips and caused her heart to skitter in her chest.

"My sister is happy to have a boy at the table who likes her cooking," he told Daniel. "You can have seconds on anything you like."

"You'll spoil him," Isaac cautioned.

"Not spoiled, but loved." Emma placed a large spoonful of mashed potatoes on his plate and a biscuit topped with a pat of butter that melted over the side of the golden roll.

"Save room for pie," she added.

"*Datt* says you make the best pies in the whole world."

Emma's cheeks pinked. She glanced shyly at Isaac. "Does he now?"

Daniel nodded. "And he's right."

Everyone at the table laughed, even Miriam. Again she

glanced at Abram and felt more than a tug at her heart. Her earlier annoyance melted like the butter on the boy's biscuit. Abram's laugh was deep and warm and engaging, making her want to stretch out her hand to touch him as if even the distance across the table kept them too far apart.

For a moment she forgot about everything except sitting across from him, enjoying the delicious meal Emma had prepared and shared with neighbors. The moment offered a reprieve of hope and warmth. If only life could remain like this forever.

Not long after that she realized her mistake when Abram hurried from the table after dinner to feed his animals and tend to his livestock. Was he fleeing from her?

Miriam washed the dishes while Emma and Isaac talked on the front porch and Daniel played nearby with Bear. She could hear his laughter as he and the dog frolicked in the front yard.

With the falling twilight, the house grew shadowed. Miriam wasn't sure when Emma wanted the gas lamps lit so she continued to wash and dry and put away the dishes by the natural light coming through the window.

A car's headlights appeared on the road, which caused her to shudder. Was Serpent coming back for her? At least Isaac was still on the property and Abram nearby. No reason for Miriam to be unsettled. But she was.

She placed the last plate on the shelf then glanced up and spied the rifle lying on top of the cupboard. Knowing it was there brought comfort.

Working quickly, she poured out the wash and rinse water and wiped her hands on the towel, ready to scurry upstairs if the car turned into the drive.

She let out a deep breath when it continued on at the fork, probably headed to Willkommen.

Emma had said the Rogers's house was four miles away

along the road that led over the river. She could easily walk that distance. If the Rogers had a computer and were connected to the internet, and if they didn't mind her using their system, she could send an email to Hannah.

Although she knew Abram wouldn't want her traipsing around the countryside, she needed to contact her sister, and if she left early enough, he might not notice she was gone.

Abram had ignored her mention of the neighbors earlier. She wouldn't bring them up again. Nor would she ask Abram to accompany her. She didn't want him exposed to danger. Instead, she could leave a note for Emma, if she could find paper and pencil.

Searching in a nearby basket of stationery, she happened upon a tablet and pencils. Ripping off a blank sheet, she took it and one of the pencils to her room.

She would need a good night's sleep so she could get up before dawn. Abram rose early. She would have to be careful so he didn't hear her.

Miriam didn't want to disturb his life any more than she already had done. Serpent was ruthless and he didn't care who he hurt. She could never forgive herself if something happened to Abram or his sister.

Her plan was to leave as early as possible in the morning. If she heard a car, she would hide in the woods.

Miriam wouldn't let Serpent find her. Not tomorrow. Not ever.

Abram couldn't sleep and it was not his wife he was thinking of as he tossed from side to side. His thoughts were on the beautiful woman who had sat across from him at dinner and kept her gaze lowered. Then Daniel had made her laugh.

The look she had shared with Abram stirred a cold place deep within him. Without stopping to think, he had laughed deeply, feeling the grief of the past slip away and a warmth and joy return that was restorative, like a spring shower or warm sunshine after a cold winter.

As much as he enjoyed the feeling, he was concerned by the ever-stronger feelings he was having for the *Englisch* woman.

What would the bishop say about Abram's actions? The bishop would probably counsel Abram to guard himself from the *fancy* woman who would move on without looking back. He would also remind Abram that the Amish remained within their faith when they married. The only way his relationship with Miriam could develop was if she joined the Amish church.

Frustrated by the dead end he seemed to be facing, Abram rose from bed, slipped on his trousers and went to the window to study the night sky. The stars twinkled, causing him a moment of melancholy. Rebecca always said the stars were a sign from those who had gone before as well as a visible sign of *Gott*'s love.

Rebecca had said many things that were not what the Amish believed, but Abram had not countered her thoughts. Tonight he wished she would tell him what to do.

A dog barked in the distance. Abram stared into the night. Something caught his gaze.

Movement?

His neck tensed. A fox stalking one of his chickens? Or something more sinister? Hopefully not the man with a serpent tattoo on his neck.

Abram left his bedroom and quietly walked downstairs and into the kitchen. There he stared out the window at where he had earlier seen movement.

Opening the back door, he slipped onto the porch and breathed in the cold night air. His gaze darted to the chicken coup and the shop, then the barn and woodshed as if daring Serpent to make a move.

Standing deathly still, Abram strained to make out the various sounds of the night. An owl hooted. A rodent scurried through the underbrush. Again, a dog barked in the distance. Abram stared into the night for a long time until the prickling in his neck eased. He saw no other movement and only heard familiar sounds he recognized.

Turning, he stepped back into the kitchen.

"He was out there?"

Miriam stood in the middle of the kitchen with a lap blanket around her shoulders, her hair hanging free.

He closed and locked the door behind him.

"I wanted fresh air," he said, hoping the excuse sounded plausible.

"I don't believe you, Abram. You heard something."

He shrugged. "I saw movement, but that does not mean I did not need fresh air as well."

"Was it Serpent?"

"I saw nothing more than a movement that could have been a fox or coyote. Even a raccoon. I doubt Serpent could remain quiet for as long as I stood on the porch. You need not worry tonight. You are safe."

"Thank you."

"For listening to the night?" he asked.

"For protecting me. I've never had anyone care about my well-being."

"Perhaps not your mother, but what of your father?"

"I never knew my father, and my mother thought more about herself than her children."

Abram heard the hurt in her voice that could not be feigned.

"I am sorry, Miriam. A father provides love and support for his children. You missed that growing up."

"I missed a lot of things that you have here."

Abram stepped closer. "You mean the farm and the picturesque landscape?"

"I mean working with your hands and turning off the world. You're not bombarded with messages and phone calls."

"Yet I have few of the things you are used to in your life."

She nodded and then stepped closer. "But do they matter?"

He touched her hair, feeling its silky softness.

Moonlight drifted through the window, spotlighting her in its glow. Her eyelids fluttered closed and her lips, full and soft, parted ever so slightly. She tipped her head.

More than anything, he longed to lower his lips to hers and drink in the softness of her skin and the heady smell of her. For one long moment Abram's stable life titled off-kilter and all he could think of was how much he wanted to kiss her.

Suddenly her eyes flew open and she drew back with a gasp. "I'm sorry."

Without offering an explanation, she turned and ran up the stairs, leaving him alone in the dark kitchen.

What was wrong with him? He never should have drawn so close to her or allowed himself such thoughts. A more righteous man would have told her to return to her room and not to worry about Serpent. Instead he had thought only of himself and his own wishes.

What did Miriam need?

She didn't need an Amish man who could only offer her hard work and little worldly recompense. He had withstood the pain of Rebecca's passing, but he could not endure seeing Miriam hurt.

Her needs came first.

Not his.

* * *

Abram's almost kiss rocked Miriam's world. All she could think of was how his lips would have felt brushed against hers as he pulled her into his arms and held her tight.

Then she'd opened her eyes, not knowing where she was or what she was supposed to do next. So she'd done the only thing that came to mind, the very thing her mother had always done when people started to get too close. Miriam fled upstairs to the protection of the guest room.

Standing with her back to the closed door, she dropped her head into her hands, expecting her heart to explode in her chest.

The near kiss had changed everything. Or had it?

The realization hit hard.

Abram hadn't been thinking of her. He had been thinking of kissing his wife.

Miriam had acted like a fickle schoolgirl. He wasn't interested in her. Why couldn't she remember that she was wearing Rebecca's clothing? The kitchen had been dark, which was even more reason for him to think of her as someone else.

She crawled into bed then jammed her fist into the pillow as she turned onto her side. Hot tears burned her eyes. Rebecca had been a lucky woman to have a strong and determined man like Abram love her so completely that even three years after her death he was still longing for his wife. Miriam felt like a fool. She would never make that mistake again.

Eventually she fell asleep only to dream about a tall Amish man who kept running from her. Why wouldn't he stop so she could talk to him? Then she saw why he kept moving forward. He was running toward a woman in the distance.

The woman glanced over her shoulder at him and smiled.

He called her name but she wouldn't stop. He called to her again and again.

The name he called out was Rebecca.

Even in her dreams, Abram was running after his deceased wife.

TEN

Miriam woke with a start. She glanced at the window and groaned, seeing the gray morning sky through the window. Why had she slept so late today of all days? She had planned to rise before sunup and leave the house at the first light of dawn. Abram was probably already up and he was the last person she wanted to run into today.

After rising from bed she quickly straightened the covers and arranged the quilt before she dressed, again in Amish garb. She was getting the hang of using straight pins to fasten the fabric and felt comfortable in the calf-length cotton just as she felt comfortable in this Amish home. Drawing in a deep breath, she opened the bedroom door and tiptoed down the stairs.

On the last step she hesitated, hearing sounds from the kitchen—the scrape of a cast-iron skillet on the stove followed by the clink of glasses and the clatter of plates.

Emma was preparing breakfast and the smell of fresh-baked biscuits wafted through the house and made Miriam's mouth water. As much as she would have enjoyed the hearty meal, Miriam needed to leave without being noticed lest Emma convince her to stay.

And Abram? Would he be relieved to have her gone?

She couldn't think about Abram with his crystal-blue eyes and full lips. She had to think about Hannah. Her sister would come to her rescue and take her to Atlanta. Surely law enforcement in the city would begin an investigation into her mother's death and Sarah's disappearance.

Miriam crossed the main room and carefully opened the front door. The hinge creaked. Her breath caught. She stopped and listened, then let out a shallow sigh as the oven banged open and a metal baking pan dropped onto the top of the stove.

Grateful her departure hadn't been noticed, Miriam slipped outside and pulled the black cape around her shoulders. She glanced at the mountain, relieved that no cars were in sight, and then scurried down the steps and across the front yard to the road that passed in front of Abram's house, the road that would take her to the Rogers's farm.

Glancing back, she looked for some sign of Abram. All she saw was the cluster of trees that blocked her view of the barn where he was probably tending to the horses. With a heavy heart, she started to run, not knowing what she would find on the road ahead. Emma had mentioned a broken bridge that was still accessible. Miriam didn't like heights and her family had never stayed anywhere long enough for her to learn to swim. If only the bridge would be sturdy enough to allow her to cross safely.

She couldn't dwell on the danger. Instead she needed to focus on accessing the internet so she could email Hannah.

A lump thickened her throat as she ran. She wouldn't see Abram again. He would go on with his farm while she made a new life for herself in Atlanta.

After the peace of the countryside, she wasn't sure city life would be to her liking. At least she would be free of Serpent and safe in Atlanta.

Yet she had felt safe with Abram, as well.

Safe from Serpent but not safe to guard her heart. Her heart was in danger with Abram, which was a different kind of problem.

If only Abram had seen who Miriam truly was instead of seeing only the dress and apron that reminded him of his wife.

Abram sensed that something was amiss.

Leaving Nellie's stall, he stared through the open breezeway, his gaze flicking across the pasture as he listened for the squawk of chickens or the neigh of one of the horses grazing in the distant pasture.

What had caused his unrest?

The kitchen door opened and Emma motioned him to the house. The thought of biscuits, sliced ham, eggs and corn mush whet his always eager appetite. An even more alluring thought was sitting across from Miriam.

He waved to Emma in response to her call then returned to the barn to add more water to the horses' troughs.

Bear rose from his bed of straw, stretched and padded forward to stand by his empty bowl.

"I haven't forgotten you." Abram poured kibble into the dog's dish and then sighed seeing the gray that tangled through Bear's once golden coat. "What happened to my watchdog? The years have passed too quickly. You are a faithful companion, but you have become fat and lazy in your old age."

Bear titled his head as if hearing the concern in his master's voice.

"We have a serpent on the loose and both of us must be on guard." Abram patted the dog's head then returned the bag of food to the storage room and hurried to the water pump.

After washing his hands, Abram entered the house, inhaling the savory aroma of biscuits and fried eggs and bacon. He glanced at the empty table.

"Our guest has not risen?" he asked his sister.

"She was tired last night, although I thought the smell of breakfast would wake her."

The rumble of a car engine sent Abram to the front of the house. He peered out the window.

Serpent's black sedan headed up the hill. Not who Abram wanted to see, not this early, not ever. The man should stay in Petersville and never set foot in Willkommen or the surrounding area, if Abram had his way.

"Who is it?" his sister called from the kitchen.

"The man with the tattoo who searches for Miriam."

Emma entered the living area and moved toward the window. "That one is an evil man."

"Perhaps. But we will let *Gott* read his heart."

"Now you are not worried about him?"

"I did not say that. But we cannot judge."

"I can voice my opinion."

Abram had to smile. Although petite and slender, Emma sometimes spoke her mind and if something troubled her, she would not be still.

"I must check on Miriam." Emma started up the stairs. "She needs to be warned that the Serpent is in the area."

Abram returned his gaze to the window. Serpent's car had disappeared around the bend in the road. Where was he going and when would he return?

Stepping onto the porch, Abram listened to the silence, hoping it would last. Emma's cry cut through the quiet and sent Abram's heart racing. He ran inside and met her at the foot of the stairway.

His sister's eyes were lined with worry. "Miriam is not in her room."

"She washed her clothes last night. Perhaps she is gathering them off the line." Abram hurried to the kitchen. "I will find her."

"I'm afraid she's gone." Emma's words followed Abram out the door. He raced to the barn.

"Miriam?" he called as he passed Bear and the horse stalls and headed to the rear doorway.

Her clothes hung on a line behind the barn, protected from the wandering eye of any person who traveled along the roadway. Emma had been particular about where she hung clothing to dry. With Serpent on the prowl, Abram was grateful for the secluded clothesline.

But at the moment, he was more interested in finding Miriam than where she had hung her clothing. He flicked his gaze left and right. His stomach roiled, realizing Emma's statement was true. Miriam was gone.

Quickly he hitched Nellie to the buggy. Emma met him outside the barn.

"Miriam asked me about any *Englisch* neighbors who might have a computer she could use to contact her sister. I told her about the Rogers."

"She mentioned them to me, as well." Worry tangled Abram's heart. "If she took the fork in the road, Serpent would have seen her. He could have captured her by now."

Emma shook her head. "I told her the road to the bridge is the fastest route."

"But the bridge is out."

"Only partially. A person on foot could traverse the crossing without problem."

"Unless the rotten wood gives way. I'm going there."

"She wants to contact her sister, Abram."

He nodded. "Perhaps that is so, but she is in danger with Serpent nearby."

The sound of a car downshifting turned Abram's gaze to the mountain. His eyes narrowed as he caught sight of lights on the roof of a black sedan.

Although he could not see the driver from this distance, he knew who was at the wheel. The realization made his blood boil.

The man with the serpent tattoo.

He was coming for Miriam.

ELEVEN

Miriam didn't like heights and she didn't like rushing water, both of which she had to face if she were to pass over the river and continue on to the Rogers's farm.

Gazing over the side of the bridge's broken guardrail made her stomach woozy as she peered at the rain-swollen water below. Sharp gusts of wind rushed across the surface of the river, forming froth and white caps.

She shivered from the cold that seeped through her cape and also from fear as she gazed into the turbulence below. Emma had said the bridge was navigable. Miriam wasn't so sure.

Two sections of the bridge platform were still standing, but the guardrails had collapsed and the entire structure appeared rickety at best.

The sound of water rushing over the rocks was as ominous as the gray skies overhead and the gathering storm clouds. The morning had started out clear and had given her hope. Now, peering at the dark clouds above and the even darker water below, her hopes were dashed. She had been foolish to leave the security of Abram's home. Walking four miles wasn't the problem, but crossing over the water on a dilapidated bridge was. The wood creaked as an even more forceful gust of wind swirled from the west.

Miriam glanced over her shoulder, longing to see Abram's farmhouse in the far distance, but the thick woods and rolling hills obscured it from sight. Fisting her hands, she fought for resolve. She couldn't rely on the protective Amish man. She had to forge on, quite literally.

Pulling in a determined breath, she mustered her courage and took a step forward. Through the broken slats, she saw the churning water. The downward drop-off caused her head to swim. She reached for a still-attached portion of the handrail and gasped when it broke under her hold. The rotten wood crashed onto the rocks below.

Her heart pounded and fear gripped her throat.

Arching her back, she raised her arms in a frantic attempt to maintain her balance.

You'll fall to your death. The warning came from within. The internal threat sent another chill to tangle along her spine and manifest in outward shivering that sucked the air from her lungs and left her gasping.

Above the roar of the water she heard a rhythmic cadence. Not a car but the *clip-clop* of a horse's hooves.

"Miriam?"

Recognizing Abram's voice, she steeled her resolve to keep moving forward. Cautiously, she took another step and then another.

Abram had come to stop her, yet he wasn't thinking of her own good. He was thinking of the other woman who had worn this dress. The woman he longed for Miriam to be.

"Kommst du hier." The guttural inflection of his voice sounded as ominous as the raging river. He was angry with her for leaving without saying goodbye.

He raised his voice. "Come here, Miriam. The bridge is weak. Crossing is too dangerous."

She waved a hand in the air, hoping he wouldn't follow her. She needed to be free of Abram. Free to find the Rogers' farm and use their computer. Technology she needed, even if Abram rejected the modern conveniences of the world.

"Turn around. Get in the buggy."

More demands that didn't take into consideration her plight.

"Go home, Abram. Tend to your farm. Live in the past with your memories."

"I live each day in the present, Miriam. But I live wisely, putting my faith in *Gott*."

"Your *Gott*, as you say, did not save your wife. He won't save me. I have to take care of myself."

Abram's silence tore through Miriam's heart. She'd hit a nerve that was too sensitive and too painful. Instantly she regretted her caustic tongue.

She had no reason to bring more pain to Abram's life. He carried enough of his own.

"I'm sorry." She turned, hoping he would see the depth of her contrition and her desire to make amends.

Another burst of wind tore along the riverbank, caught her full skirt and caused it to billow out around her legs. The strength of the blast of air threw her completely off balance. Suddenly the trees, the broken bridge and the water below swirled around her.

"Abram!" she screamed as she started to topple off the bridge.

Her fall was aborted by Abram's strong hands that gripped her tightly and pulled her into the safety of his embrace.

She gasped, thinking they both would tumble into the water. He pulled her even closer and lifted her into his arms.

"No," she moaned. "Let me go."

"Do as I say." He swept her off the bridge and carried her to his buggy.

She fought against his hold. He had saved her from the river, but she couldn't return to his farm.

"Shh," he soothed. "You must be quiet."

"I will not be silent." She struggled to free herself from his hold.

"It is for your own good," he warned.

"You cannot control me."

"This I know to be true, Miriam. But you must listen and comply. Do you not hear the car? He is coming to find you."

Miriam stilled and turned her face toward the sound, somewhat muffled and hard to distinguish over the tumbling water and the wind rustling through the trees.

The sky overhead darkened even more. Her stomach tightened. She knew what the sound of the engine meant. Serpent was coming after her.

If he found her, he wouldn't let her live to escape again.

Relieved that he had successfully tucked Miriam into the rear of the buggy moments earlier, Abram now stood next to Nellie and watched Serpent's car screech to a halt at the edge of the road. The swollen river pounded over the rocks and rushed under the bridge. Overhead the sky darkened with an approaching storm that appeared to be as volatile as the man climbing from his car.

"Stop where you are." Serpent's voice was laced with anger.

"What do you want?" Abram demanded.

"I want the woman in the buggy with you. I saw her foot as she climbed in. You've been hiding Miriam Miller somewhere near your farm."

"I am not sure the woman you speak of has done anything wrong."

"She's a suspected murderer and you're a fool to believe anything she says otherwise."

Serpent pulled a weapon from his waistband. "Tell her to step down from the buggy or I'll start shooting."

"Then you will be a killer."

"I'll kill you if you stop me from apprehending her."

He cocked his gun and aimed it at the buggy.

Abram started walking toward Serpent.

"Wait, my brother."

He turned at the sound of Emma's voice and, although concerned for her well-being, he was grateful his sister had insisted on coming with him. She climbed from the buggy.

"I do not understand why you needed to see me, sir." Emma's voice was calm and engaging as she stared at Serpent. "Surely, I have done nothing to cause you upset."

The man's face twisted. He glanced from Abram to Emma.

"Put down your gun," Abram demanded.

Serpent shook his head. "I don't know what kind of tricks you and your sister are playing, Zook, but I'm convinced you know where the woman is hiding. She's a criminal, and if you help her escape, you'll be prosecuted and sent to jail, along with your sister."

His gaze flickered to the surrounding countryside. "I searched your farm last night."

Abram's instincts had been right after all.

"She might not be holed up on your property," Serpent continued, "but I'm convinced she's hiding someplace not far from here. I'll keep watching, and if you make a misstep, it will be your last."

"You do not frighten me."

"That's because of your false Amish pride. But pride can't stop a bullet and pride can't make a woman come back to life. Tell the woman you're protecting that I'm coming after her. And tell your Amish friends that if they're hiding her, I'll send them to jail. The bottom line is that I'll find her, Zook." He started to get into his car and then added, "Next time she won't get away."

"I can't stay with you any longer," Miriam insisted from the rear of the buggy once Serpent's car had disappeared from sight.

Abram helped Emma into the front seat and climbed in beside her.

"Serpent was ready to kill both of you when he thought I was hiding in the buggy," Miriam continued. "As gracious as you were, Emma, to confront him, you were putting yourself in danger. What would have happened if he had stepped closer and found me hiding in the rear?"

Tears welled up in Miriam's eyes. She couldn't let any harm come to Abram and Emma. "Take me to the Rogers's house. I'll email my sister and wait for her there."

"Mr. Rogers and his wife are visiting their daughter in Nashville." Abram grabbed the reins. "They will not be home until next week."

Emma glanced back at Miriam. "I'm sorry, I did not know about their trip." Her voice was filled with regret. "I never thought you would try to find their farm alone. You should have told us what you needed."

But she had told them she needed to contact her sister. Neither Abram nor Emma realized what was at stake. If Serpent was part of a trafficking ring, the whole county would be impacted negatively by his criminal activity.

"We should all leave here and go someplace safe," Miriam suggested. "Come with me to Atlanta."

Abram grunted and flipped the reins, causing the horse

to increase her speed. "A farm must be maintained. I cannot leave my animals."

"Just until I can tell my story to honest lawmen who will come after Serpent."

"Samuel will return to Willkommen tomorrow, Miriam. We will go to town for the market. You can talk to him then."

But would he believe her story?

Miriam rubbed her forehead, hoping to ease the pounding headache that had started while she was on the bridge.

Jammed into the rear of the buggy, she felt lost. Would she ever get to Atlanta? Yet leaving meant saying goodbye to Abram, which was the last thing she wanted to do.

TWELVE

On the way back to the house Abram kept a sharp eye on the road and listened for Serpent's car. He needed to keep Miriam out of sight and out of the vile man's grasp until his uncle returned to Willkommen.

Pulling into the drive, Abram hopped out of the buggy and closed the gate behind them. Usually it stood open to welcome all. Under the circumstances, Abram needed to use any means to keep Serpent at bay. A gate was not much of a barrier, but it would stop unwanted visitors from driving directly to the house.

"I do not want to raise my hand against another man, but Serpent must be stopped," Abram mumbled to himself after the women had hurried into the house. "I will not let him harm Miriam or Emma."

Hopefully, *Gott* would provide the protection they needed so Abram could maintain his desire for good and still hide Miriam's whereabouts. From what Serpent had said, it sounded as if he thought Miriam was holed up someplace away from the farm, for which Abram was grateful.

The storm clouds that had grown darker over the morning at the river's edge now turned the day into night. His trusty dog trotted to greet him as he unhitched Nellie in the barn and quickly groomed her.

"Remember the serpent, Bear. We must be vigilant and ensure he does no harm." Once Nellie was settled in her stall, Abram hurried to the house, but he could not outrun the downpour. The sky opened and the rain fell with fury.

The walkway turned to mud and caught at Abram's footsteps. Lightening cut across the menacing sky followed by a deafening roar of thunder.

He stomped his feet on the porch to loosen the mud from his boots before he stepped into the warmth and comfort of his kitchen.

Miriam stood at the dry sink with her back to him, her skirts full around her legs. She appeared to be beating batter in a bowl.

For a moment his heart stopped, thinking it was Rebecca. Then she turned and he was struck again by the reality of who had changed his life.

The woman at the dry sink was not his wife. She was Miriam with her troubled gaze and eyes that studied him far too deeply as if always questioning his reaction.

He could not let her know the way his heart lurched and his lungs constricted, making each breath difficult when he was around her.

He was not thinking of his wife or the past, which is what Miriam had mentioned in her anger at the river's edge. He was thinking of this newcomer to his life who had shattered his *plain* world and caused him to think thoughts of a new beginning and hope for the future. But she was not interested in an Amish man who disavowed all the technology and electrical devices she was used to having in her *Englisch* world. Nor was she interested in embracing his Amish faith, which meant there could be no future for them. Abram was a fool to allow his heart to have dominance over his reasoning.

He steeled his gaze and pulled in a deep breath, struggling to maintain a firm control of his voice and his actions. He had to be strong and assertive to guard his heart and his life.

He didn't need Miriam to disrupt the status quo and cause him to think of what could be. What could be was not reality, and Abram lived in the real world. A world of hard work and faith in *Gott*. A world where family came first and the *Englisch* ways were kept from polluting the serenity of the Amish life.

Miriam would never understand him or his ways, which meant there was no hope for them. Ever.

End of subject.

"You're wet, Abram. I will make coffee. Sit by the fire to get warm."

Her sincere concern caused another knife to jab at his heart. Her voice was smooth as honey and equally as sweet, and the firm resolve that he had convinced himself was necessary suddenly crumbled. All he wanted was to pull her into his arms, as he had done at the bridge when he had feared she would fall into the water.

Had she felt the erratic pounding of his heart? Did she know how much he longed to have her in his arms again?

Silly, foolish feelings that were not to be allowed.

Without so much as a word, he walked past her and hurried up the stairs to his bedroom. The room where he and his wife had shared the joys of wedded life, but also the room where her life had ended along with the baby's. *The Lord giveth life and the Lord taketh life away.*

And now?

Was the Lord giving Abram a new life? Or was he ripping out his heart and sucking the very breath from him so that nothing in the future would ever compare with Miriam?

Abram slammed the bedroom door behind him and

reached for his Bible. The scriptures had comforted him after Rebecca's death.

Would he find comfort from the readings now? Or would even the Word of *Gott* bring added confusion?

Why had Miriam sought refuge in Abram's arms when she was running from Serpent?

Abram knew the reason.

Gott had known his loneliness and had longed to bring comfort, but instead of comfort, Miriam's presence had brought chaos and tumult.

"Forgive me." Abram shook his head as he prayed. "I know not what to do."

The kitchen grew dark, making Miriam long for electricity and lights. Emma stood at the stove, stirring red sauce, seemingly unaware of the dark skies and pounding rain that thrummed against the tin roof. The downpour grew in intensity. Thunder roared and lightning flashed through the darkness with bursts of brightness.

Miriam shivered, chilled by the fury of the storm.

"We are safe here in the house," Emma assured her, no doubt seeing Miriam grimace as each roll of thunder rumbled overhead.

"I don't like storms," she stated emphatically.

"Rain is good for the land. Abram will till the fields soon. The rain will help to soften the soil."

"Rain doesn't bother me, but lightning and thunder do."

Emma glanced out the window. Miriam followed her gaze. Visibility was worse than poor, making the barn and pastures beyond blurred by the downpour.

"You would still be walking to the Rogers' home if Abram had not taken the buggy to find you."

Miriam looked at the Amish woman. "I appreciate his thoughtfulness."

Emma added salt to the sauce. "You do not understand Amish men."

Miriam raised her brow. "I don't know what you mean."

"An Amish man is proud. He works hard. He takes care of his family, his wife, his children. He is the leader of the family. He embraces the Word of *Gott* and lives by the teachings of Christ."

"*Englisch* men do the same. At least, some of them."

"Perhaps, but Amish men commit totally to the women they love."

"Good men exist outside the Amish community," Miriam insisted. Yet the one man who had broken through her guarded heart *was* Amish.

Miriam swallowed the lump that formed in her throat. "You don't have to spell out what you're trying to tell me."

The Amish woman raised a brow. "You understand then?"

"I understand Abram still loves his wife."

Emma shook her head. "Then you don't understand."

Miriam sighed with exasperation. "What are you trying to say, Emma?"

"Do you see the way he looks at you?"

"Of course, and I know why. I'm wearing his wife's clothing. He looks at me with longing because he longs for Rebecca."

Emma harrumphed. "Is that what you think? I noticed that you washed your clothing, but they were hanging outside and got wet in the rain. I moved them into the barn to dry."

"Thank you. I wasn't thinking."

"Just like you aren't thinking correctly about Abram. Wear your *fancy* clothes and see how he looks at you then."

"I wouldn't call my jeans and sweater fancy."

"*Fancy* is a term we Amish use for anything other than our *plain* clothing. You understand? It is an expression, *yah*? But you talk around my comment."

"You mean Abram won't look at me at all if I wear regular clothes?"

Emma shook her head and sighed. "It is not something we need to discuss further. Our midday meal must be cooked."

Miriam didn't understand the sharpness of Emma's tone. She sounded as if she was accusing Miriam of being the one at fault.

How could that be? Miriam had done nothing to provoke Abram or his sister. All too quickly she realized her mistake. Miriam had brought tumult and danger to their peaceful lives.

THIRTEEN

The sound of a car engine forced Abram to gaze from his bedroom window. The deputy sheriff's squad car pulled into the drive. Curtis Idler braked to a stop, left the dryness of his car and opened the gate. Rain drenched him in seconds. His face seemed twisted with frustration as he climbed back into his car and drove into the yard. He parked near the back porch and eyed the sky through the window. The rain eased and he took the opportunity to leave the protection of his car and run to the porch.

He banged on the door.

"Abram?" Emma called from the first floor.

Racing downstairs, Abram passed his sister and hurried into the kitchen. Miriam had backed into the pantry, her eyes wide with worry.

"It is the deputy from town. My uncle trusts him. Perhaps you should too."

"No, Abram. I can't."

"You have nothing to fear, Miriam."

"Not today. I'll wait until your uncle returns."

He did not understand her hesitancy when she had been so eager to go to town.

"Please, Abram." Her eyes pleaded with him. "I can't explain my feelings, but don't make me talk to anyone now."

She glanced at the kitchen door as once again the deputy knocked, demanding entrance.

"Hurry upstairs," Abram said, seeing the worry that tightened her face. "I will call you when he is gone."

Gathering her skirts in her hands, she ran from the room. Her footfalls sounded as she climbed the stairs. The click of the bedroom door closing gave a sense of finality to her departure.

"Get coffee," Abram told Emma. "The deputy is wet from the rain."

Opening the door, he motioned the man inside. Idler wiped his feet on the braided rug Rebecca had made and stepped toward the table.

"Coffee sounds perfect," Curtis said after Abram had made the offer. "The rain's coming down so hard I couldn't see."

"You are far from town." Abram stated the obvious.

Emma poured a cup of coffee and placed it on the table in front of the lawman.

"There is fresh cream and sugar." She pointed to the cream pitcher and bowl of sugar on the table.

He shook his head. "Black is fine. I didn't come for refreshment."

Abram accepted a cup from his sister, took a long pull of the hot brew and eyed the deputy, waiting for him to divulge the reason for this second visit within two days.

"Sheriff Kurtz isn't sure he'll get back to town tomorrow. He put me in charge until he returns."

"What about the roadblock?" Abram asked. "Has it not been successful?"

"That was Chief Tucker's idea."

"The chief of police from Petersville?"

Curtis nodded. "He's convinced the killer is still in the area and wants to do a house-by-house search."

Abram bristled. He placed his cup on the table and

pulled in a breath before he spoke. "Even I know that a warrant would be required prior to a house search. Does the sheriff think of himself as above the law? From what I have heard, it sounds as if the man has a high opinion of himself."

"You don't understand, Abram."

"I understand enough to know he will not find welcome here."

"He's going to search all the Amish homes," Curtis said.

"Doors will not open to the chief or his men."

"Here's the thing, Abram. A killer's on the loose. You folks are in danger. I'm trying to tell as many of the Amish as I can."

"This supposed killer is the woman whose photograph was on your phone? You think she killed her mother?"

"That's right. But without transportation, she would be hard-pressed to leave the area."

"Have you forgotten the bus that comes to Willkommen? She could have gone north to Knoxville or south to Atlanta."

"Except the clerk at the bus station hasn't seen anyone matching her description. He knows most folks in town."

"But he does not know all the Amish."

Curtis nodded. "You're right, although I don't think the killer is Amish."

"Someone could have driven her," Abram suggested, hoping the search would shift to some other portion of the state.

"That's a possibility, if she knew someone in the area."

"Has anyone seen her?"

"Not a soul." The deputy took a long swig of coffee and then wiped his lips and sniffed. "I'm sure you've kept your eyes open."

"I have seen a surly man with a scarf around his neck."

Idler smirked. "You're talking about Pete Pearson. He can be pushy to say the least."

"I do not want him prowling around my property. If you see him, tell him to leave the Amish alone. We do not need his protection or his accusations, and we do not want to face a roadblock the days we go to market."

Curtis held up his hand. "The roadblock ends tonight. The Petersville mayor refuses to pay any more overtime to his police officers. However, squad cars will be patrolling the roadways and officers will be on the lookout for the woman on the run."

"Are you searching for the right person?" Abram asked.

"We've got one lead, Abram, and it seems sound. Keep your eyes open and let me know if you see anything suspect."

The deputy rose and handed Emma his empty cup. "Appreciate the coffee."

A floorboard creaked overhead. The deputy glanced up. "Someone visiting?"

Emma smiled sweetly. "The mice have been bad this year. We brought one of our cats inside. She is a good mouser who is growing fat and causing the floors to creak when she leaps from the bed."

"Only rodent I like," the deputy snarled, "is a dead one."

He nodded to Abram. "See you in town."

Emma frowned at Abram when the deputy was not looking.

Abram raised his brow at her. "I'm sure Deputy Idler would enjoy an Amish dessert with his supper this evening. Especially after he was so considerate to warn us, Emma. Didn't you mention having an extra apple pie?"

Thankfully her face melted into a smile. "The pie is in the pantry. I'll wrap it in cheesecloth for protection from the rain."

The deputy slapped Abram's shoulder. "Thanks for your thoughtfulness."

Emma hurried to the pantry and returned with the pie.

"You folks stay safe." The deputy held the pie close to his chest and scurried to his car.

Abram closed and locked the kitchen door.

"Can we trust him, Abram?" Emma asked, her face pensive, her arms wrapped protectively around her waist.

"We can trust him as much as we can trust anyone at this point. The pie will keep his mind off the creaking floorboards and the cat we never allow in the house."

As the car pulled out of the drive and turned onto the main road, heading back to town, Bear started to bark.

Abram shook his head at his lazy watchdog's poor timing before he called up the stairs to Miriam. "The deputy is gone."

She came to the top of the landing. "I can't stay here, Abram. I have to leave. I'm a danger to you and Emma."

"The roadblock ends tonight. We will go to Willkommen in the morning. There we will find more information. Perhaps we will find your aunt."

"I need a computer to email my sister."

Abram nodded. "We will find that, as well. But tonight you must remain here. You are safe with me."

At least, he hoped she was.

The day seemed to last forever or perhaps it was Miriam's unease that made time tick by so slowly.

She'd started the morning nearly falling into a raging river. Moments later she'd eluded Serpent, thanks to Abram's quick reaction. The Willkommen deputy's visit some hours later, along with the stormy sky and intermittent rain, had fueled her anxiety even more. Now with the lunch meal over and the dishes washed and put away in the cupboard, she wondered how to endure the rest of the afternoon.

Emma seemed as flustered as Miriam felt.

"I'm worried about Daniel," the Amish woman said as

she headed once again to the front window and peered in the direction of the Beiler dairy. "He usually brings milk soon after our *middaagesse*."

Miriam came up behind her and patted her arm.

Emma smiled weakly. "I should have said our noon meal. Why has he not yet brought the day's milk?"

"Perhaps his delay is due to the storm," Miriam offered.

"Suppose the boy is sick? He does not have a *Mamm*, and Isaac must tend to his dairy cows. The child would be alone, perhaps feverish—"

"You're jumping far ahead of things, Emma. I'm sure there's an explanation for why he's late that has nothing to do with illness."

Emma nodded and slowly turned away from the window. "Still I worry. The child is always punctual. He will start school in the next session. I will miss seeing him each day."

"Isaac will deliver the milk instead," Miriam added with a wink.

"You have been with us a short time, Miriam Miller, yet you see into the heart of things."

Miriam smiled. "I see your heart that is filled with love for Isaac."

Emma shook her head as if wanting no such talk in spite of the twinkle in her eyes. "I will bake cookies. That is one way to attract Daniel. Even with this distance between the two farms, he is drawn to the sweet smell of my baking."

As Emma hurried into the kitchen, Miriam returned to the window. She wouldn't tell Emma, but she, too, worried about the young boy on the road with Serpent making his presence known so frequently. As much as she wanted to believe the hateful man would not bother a child, there was nothing she would put past Serpent.

A chill settled over her and she shivered. Rubbing her arms, she stared into the distance wondering where the snake was hiding. He was out there somewhere, watching and waiting.

Reluctantly she joined Emma in the kitchen, but her heart wasn't in the baking. She peered through the kitchen window to where Abram mended the fence that cordoned off a distant pasture. A cold wind blew from the north and caused his shirt to billow in the gusty air. He worked without his coat and with only his wide-brimmed hat to shield his face from the buffeting rain.

Before the first batch of cookies went into the oven, Emma glanced at the kitchen clock and headed once again to the front room. Gazing through the window, she groaned.

"The rain has eased, which is good, and I see Daniel, but he is carrying three bottles of milk instead of the regular two. The load is much too heavy." She tsked and shook her head. "The boy thinks he is older than his years."

Miriam peered around Emma. "He means to please and works hard like his father."

"*Yah*, but his father does not carry more than he can haul. I fear Daniel will drop one of the bottles, if not all three."

Turning her gaze to the mountain road, Miriam's heart thumped a warning. "Emma, look, it's the black sedan."

Serpent was heading down the hill.

Emma's hand drew to her throat. "I must help Daniel and bring him inside."

She pushed past Miriam, but with the rain-slick roadway and her labored gait, Emma would never get to the boy in time.

"Stay in the house," Miriam insisted. "I'll go instead."

"But Serpent—"

"Daniel and I will be safely inside before he could see us."

Without waiting for Emma to express any more of her concerns, Miriam pushed open the front door. She unlatched the gate and ran to where the young boy stood, trying to readjust his heavy load.

"Daniel, let me help you."

"I can do it," he insisted, clutching two of the bottles close to his chest. The third bottle teetered in his outstretched hand and seemed ready to slip through his fingers.

"Of course you can, but we must hurry. Emma is baking cookies. They are almost done."

She glanced at the sedan. Her pulse raced, seeing the car accelerate even faster down the hill. "Hurry, Daniel."

Taking two of the milk bottles in her right hand, she grabbed the boy's free hand with her left and hurried him along.

Looking over her shoulder, her heart stopped. The car was close. So very close.

Dropping the bottles, she lifted Daniel into her arms.

"Die millich—!" he cried.

"We must hurry, Daniel." She tucked his head into the crook of her neck to protect the child and ran for the house.

Tires screeched. A car door slammed. "Stop."

She wouldn't stop. She had to get the child to safety. Racing up the steps of the porch, she gasped with relief as the door opened. Miriam clutched the boy even closer to her heart and sprinted into the house.

Emma slammed and locked the door behind them. Taking Daniel into her arms, she kissed his cheek and pulled him into her embrace. "Oh, Daniel, we were so worried about you."

"Die millich...the bottles broke." Tears welled up in the boy's eyes.

"Yes, but you are safe."

Serpent climbed the porch steps and pounded on the door.

Emma scooted the boy into the kitchen. "Hide, Daniel, in the pantry."

"He frightens me." Daniel's voice was tight with fear.

"I know, but you must be very brave." Emma hurried him into the hiding place. "We will not let the man hurt you."

Miriam reached on top of the cupboard and grabbed Abram's rifle. Returning to the living area, she stood behind the door next to Emma and nodded.

Gripping the knob, Emma opened the door ever so slightly. "Why are you here?"

"I saw a woman with a boy."

"I was that woman," Emma insisted, her voice calm but firm. "My brother told you to leave us alone."

Miriam's heart thumped. She nudged Emma and shoved the rifle into her hand.

"I don't care what Zook said." Serpent gloated.

Emma raised the rifle. "You *should* listen to Abram."

A dog barked.

Miriam glanced through the narrow crack on the hinged side of the door. Bear ran to the front of the house and scurried up the porch to snap at Serpent's feet.

"Get that hound away from me."

"Pearson!" Abram appeared, his face twisted in anger. "Why do you trespass on my land?"

"You can't scare me, Zook."

Bear bared his teeth and lunged. Serpent tried to kick the dog, but Bear eluded the blow.

"Leave my property and don't come back," Abram's voice was deep and menacing.

"You'll pay for this, Zook." Serpent stumbled down the steps and raced to his car.

Emma closed the door and grabbed Miriam's hand. Tears pooled in Emma's eyes. "When will it end?"

Miriam knew. It would end when she was out of Emma and Abram's home. Only then would the peace of their Amish life return.

FOURTEEN

The rain intensified through the night. The *ping* of the fat droplets against the tin roof kept Miriam from sleeping. She walked to the window and stared into the darkness and shivered, knowing who could be out there waiting and watching.

Closing the curtains, she lit the gas lamp and opened the trunk. The dress she had worn today was spattered with mud. Tomorrow she would wear something fresh to town. The smell of cedar from the inlaid wood brought comfort.

She peered at the inscription, handwritten in black ink, on the inside. *To Rebecca. With my love. From your husband, Abram.*

Miriam's heart constricted. Not with jealousy or envy, but because of her own desire to have someone love her as completely as Abram had loved his wife.

Tears burned her eyes, knowing the pain of loss he must have felt when Rebecca and their child had died. He continued to carry that pain, Miriam felt sure. The look of longing in his eyes revealed the depth of his grief, even now.

Wiping her hand across her cheek, she inhaled deeply to quell the onslaught of sadness that clung to her as surely as the scent of cedar.

Miriam pulled a dress from the trunk. This one in a

deep royal blue that almost seemed too rich for an Amish woman. She shook out the fabric and held the bodice against her, then looked down at the skirt that billowed around her legs in a graceful flow that made her feel totally feminine.

She twirled once. Yards of fabric swirled around her legs and, in spite of her heavy heart, she smiled, feeling as graceful as a fairy princess with the skirt swishing back and forth. She almost laughed, until the light flickered, drawing her back to the moment. She wasn't Abram's wife. She was a stranger who had barged into his life. A stranger who had dreamed thoughts of what could have been—of love and marriage, a home and family—all of which Miriam would never know.

A man's love and affection were not in her future. She was her mother's daughter, as much as she wanted to break the generational ties. Yet she would not walk the same path as her mother, who had needed a man to validate her life.

Miriam didn't need a man.

But you want one, her mind taunted. *An Amish man who is bigger than life.*

A door opened into the hallway. Footsteps sounded then stopped outside her door. Miriam's heart lunged. She clasped the dress to her heart, wanting to hide it from sight as if Abram could see through the closed bedroom door and know her thoughts.

She held her breath and looked at the gas lamp. Abram would see the light spilling into the dark hallway from under the bedroom door, and he would know she was awake.

Her right hand raised to cover her mouth as she slowly exhaled the air that burned her lungs, half expecting him to open the door and demand to know why she was holding his wife's dress.

Again she was overcome with regret. She never should have infringed on Abram's life.

Another footfall and another. Abram passed her door and descended the stairs to the first floor.

Daring not move for fear a floorboard would squeak, she listened to the trail of his footsteps through the house. The back door creaked open and then closed.

She extinguished the light, moved to the window and pulled back the curtain. The rain continued to fall. Overhead the moon peered between billowing clouds to illuminate the yard ever so slightly.

Miriam could see Abram walk to the woodshop. He held something in his hand. A chill settled over her. He held the rifle.

Stamping his feet, he entered the shop and then pulled the door closed behind him.

Without his presence in the house, she felt an instant dread. Again her eyes searched the land around the house and outbuildings.

A shadow moved near the woodshed.

Her heart lurched.

Had she imagined the movement or was someone hiding in the darkness?

Sleep had eluded Abram. He had been restless and unable to calm his mind or his heart. Needing to busy himself, he had come to the workshop, planning to sand a table he was making for Emma.

That he had brought the rifle surprised him somewhat, yet his sister had used it this afternoon when Serpent had chased after Miriam and Daniel. Abram had been almost too late returning to the house. Thankfully, Serpent had driven away. Next time, he might not be so easily deterred.

For a long moment Abram stared into the dark recesses

of the woodshop and sensed the intruder's presence before he heard the crack of a broken twig outside. Peering through the window, he saw the shadowy figure slink around the side of the woodshed.

A stocky man. Maybe six feet tall. He could not see his face, but he knew it was Serpent.

The man continued along the edge of the building then stopped and peered up at the bedroom windows. Abram angled his gaze toward the house, relieved that the light in Miriam's room had been extinguished. Just so she would remain inside.

Abram reached for the rifle. Holding it in one hand, he slowly opened the door to his shop and stepped into the cool night air. The rain had slackened to a light drizzle. He peered through the mist and angled his head, listening for a footfall to identify Serpent's whereabouts.

A twig snapped.

Abram turned to see the man dart into the clearing.

The back door opened.

Someone stepped onto the porch.

Miriam.

Abram's gut tightened.

Serpent pulled something from his waistband. The moonlight reflected off the object.

Abram's heart stopped at the sight of the handgun.

"No!" he screamed.

Serpent turned toward Abram, standing in the darkness. "Where's the woman hiding, Zook?"

"I told you to stay away from me, my sister, my farm and—"

Before Abram could complete the warning, the intruder took aim and fired. A muffled rapport. The man was using a silencer.

The bullet pinged off the nearby water pump.

"I'll kill you, Zook, but I'll kill your sister first." He fired again, this time at the shadowed figure standing on the porch.

Abram's breath caught in his throat. He raised the rifle and fired. Bear raced from the barn, growling with teeth bared. He lunged at Serpent. The man turned, nearly tripping over his feet as he ran, cursing, into the night.

"Abram?" Miriam's voice, laced with fright. She fled back into the house.

He ran forward, his heart thumping at what he might find. After entering the kitchen, he closed and locked the door and propped the rifle against the wall, all the while searching the darkness with his gaze.

"Miriam," he called, fearing the worst and praying he was wrong.

He raced into the main room where he found her slumped over the stairs. In three long strides he was at her side, pulling her into his arms. His hands touched her neck, her cheeks, her waist, searching for a gaping hole or blood that would confirm she was hurt.

"You are injured?" he asked, fearing her answer.

She gasped for air. Tears fell from her eyes.

"You were hurt?" Abram restated his question. Why did she not answer him?

His hands wove into her hair, not the bun that she usually wore, but long, flowing locks that fell around her shoulders.

Moonlight filtered through the nearby window and bathed them in its glow.

"Tell me you are all right," he demanded, his voice insistent.

"I'm…" She tried to speak. "I'm not hurt. The bullet whizzed past me. I could feel the force of its momentum, but the round did not strike me. At first I couldn't understand what had happened. The sound was muffled. I thought gunfire was louder?"

"He used a silencer." Unable to think of what he would have done if she had been injured, Abram pulled her close and silently gave thanks.

He did not deserve *Gott*'s blessings, but Miriam did not deserve *Gott*'s condemnation.

"You might not have recognized him," she said, her voice low and filled with emotion. "The moon peered from the clouds as he approached the house. I saw his face. It was Serpent."

"He mentioned my sister." Abram tried to reassure her. "Serpent thought Emma was on the porch. He wanted to kill her to get back at me."

"But I was the target, Abram."

"What happened?" As if hearing her name, Emma came to the top of the stairs, holding an oil lamp. Her face was puffy with sleep yet pulled tight with concern as she stared down at them.

"Serpent came back," Miriam said, staring into Abram's eyes. "He nearly killed me once. He tried to kill me again."

FIFTEEN

Morning came too early for Miriam. Emma rapped at her bedroom door before the first light of dawn. "Breakfast is almost ready."

Miriam rubbed her eyes and tried to wipe away the grogginess that hung on after her restless night. Sleep had eluded her. She had heard Abram pace through the house, no doubt, standing guard lest Serpent return. Abram's vigilance had put her even more on edge, knowing that Serpent could still be nearby. More than anything, she longed to erase everything that had happened and fall into a deep sleep.

Then she remembered today was market day. That meant a trip to Willkommen where she could find an internet connection and contact Hannah. She also hoped to find information about her aunt. If Sheriff Kurtz was back in town, she would tell him what had happened so he could arrest Serpent and throw the wicked man in jail.

Slipping from bed, she donned the fresh blue dress she had found in the trunk. After pulling her hair into a bun, she put on the white *kapp* Emma had showed her how to wear and an apron.

The rich aroma of fresh-baked biscuits assailed her as she entered the kitchen. Coffee perked on the stove.

Emma smiled in greeting. "The dress fits you well."

"I found it in the trunk." Miriam ran her hand over the full skirt. "Will it upset Abram to see me wearing this dress?"

"His thoughts are on the present, Miriam. He will not notice the dress but rather the woman wearing the dress."

The comment took Miriam aback. Her heart fluttered as she hurried to the kitchen door. "I'll get the milk from outside."

She stopped short before she grabbed the doorknob, thinking of what had happened last night and the bullet that had been too close.

"Stay here," Emma cautioned. "Abram will bring the milk when he returns from the barn. I'm sure he wants you to remain inside for your own safety."

Miriam appreciated Abram's concern for her well-being and thought again of his embrace last night. He had held her tight, his heart beating rapidly in his chest. Foolish though it was, Miriam hadn't wanted to leave his arms.

A knock sounded at the kitchen door. Miriam eyed Emma.

"It's Abram," his sister assured her. "Will you open the door? His hands are probably full with the milk and butter."

Miriam pulled back the curtain that covered the window and peered out just to be sure. Her heart thumped in response to Abram's handsome face that stared at her through the glass. Just as Emma had said, he carried a jug of milk in one hand and a glass container of butter in the other.

"Sorry," she said as she threw open the door. "I wanted to be certain it was you."

He stepped inside, bringing in fresh morning air and the scent of the outdoors. "That was wise after last night."

She closed and locked the door behind him.

Emma, her hand poised over a skillet of scrambled eggs,

stared at both of them. "This man is even worse than we first believed. He must be stopped."

Abram nodded in agreement. "That is why Miriam will talk to Samuel. He will track down Serpent and arrest him."

"If only he can find any other men who are involved." Emma spoke the words that troubled Miriam.

So much depended on today and how the sheriff would respond to the information she planned to provide.

Emma's brow lifted as she raised the skillet off the stove. "You are sure Samuel will be back in Willkommen today?"

Abram poured himself a cup of coffee and one for Miriam, which she gladly accepted.

"Samuel planned to be gone three days, but Curtis mentioned that the sheriff could be delayed longer. We will find out when we get to town."

"Daniel asked yesterday if he could ride to market with us." Emma plated the food. "I told him we could not give him a ride. I am concerned about the boy's safety in case anything happens."

"Because of me." Miriam gave voice to what Emma had failed to mention. "My presence here puts all of you in danger."

"It is not because of you," Emma quickly explained. "You are an innocent victim, Miriam. Serpent is the one at fault."

"Emma is right," Abram insisted. "The serpent is the problem. He could make more trouble. If so, we do not want Daniel to be caught in the conflict."

"That's what I told Isaac," Emma said with a nod. "He is worried about our safety, but he is especially concerned for his son."

"*Yah*, I do not blame Isaac." Abram refilled his cup. "The boy is precocious and smart as a whip."

"He's stolen my heart," Miriam said.

Emma placed the plates on the table. "Mine, as well."

"We will see him later today when Isaac comes to town. Daniel is never far from his father's side," Abram stated.

"Isaac seems like a nice man," Miriam mused, watching Emma's expression soften with the mention of the neighbor's name.

"Yet—" Abram took a long pull from his coffee "—Isaac does not keep the Old Order."

Emma put her hands on her hips. "We are not still in Ethridge."

"The old ways were good ways," he insisted.

"Then perhaps you should have stayed in Tennessee."

Miriam had never seen Emma so determined to make a point or so vocal. Her frustration with her brother was evident as she threw the biscuits in a basket and set them on the table.

As if trying to ignore Emma's outburst, Abram pointed Miriam to the table. "We must eat now."

They each took their seats and bowed their heads as he offered a prayer. "*Gott*, we give thanks for the food You provide and for our ability to farm the land and prepare this meal. May the work of our hands give honor to You. Amen."

The tension remained taut as they ate in silence. Once finished, Abram rose from the table. "It is time to pack the buggy. The road is long and we must get to market in time to unload and set up our stall."

Miriam hadn't finished her breakfast, but thinking about what they might face later today had taken away her appetite. Emma's eyes were downcast and she toyed with her food. Was she upset with Miriam for disrupting their lives?

"I'll wash the dishes, Emma. I'm sure you need to help

Abram load the buggy." After grabbing her plate and silverware, Miriam hurried to the sink.

Abram left the table and headed for the door. "I will hitch Nellie and bring the buggy to the side of the house."

The door slammed behind him, causing Miriam's heart to lunge in her chest. "I'm sorry, Emma."

"He is not angry with you, Miriam, he is angry with himself. He fights an inner battle. My brother holds on to the past, yet we know when things are gripped too tightly, they sometimes break. Abram feels his life shattering around him."

"I did it. Coming here was a mistake."

Emma placed her plate on the counter and gently touched Miriam's arm. "Abram struggled to follow the Amish way in his youth. He made mistakes, as we often do."

Miriam thought of her own mistake in driving her mother and sister to Georgia.

"Our father is not one to easily forgive," Emma continued. "Abram embraces the old ways in hopes of redeeming himself in our father's eyes. Yet nothing can remain as it once was. Life is a process. No one stays an infant. Growth and change are a part of life just as life and death are part of the cycle."

Looking down at the dress she wore, Miriam regretted the role she played in Abram's struggle. "I have opened old wounds and caused his grief to return anew."

"It is not you," Emma assured her. "Abram needs to forgive himself. Right now he thinks only of his pain. That is self-seeking. He is a better man than that. You have allowed him to dream of what could be. That frightens him. He is not ready to leave the world of grief and guilt he has created."

Emma's words were as confusing as the Amish way.

Abram's life never would have changed if Miriam hadn't collapsed on his front porch.

She had questioned why she hadn't gone somewhere else. The neighbor's perhaps. Although other than Isaac's dairy, there were no other homes for miles. What if she hadn't found Abram? She would have wandered through the dark and never come upon a safe refuge.

But Abram's house had been lit; she'd seen the light in the window that had beckoned her. The middle of the night, yet an Amish house had light? She reached for Emma's plate. Had that light been a sign from the Lord so she would find her way?

She shivered, thinking of Serpent following close behind her. She had been exhausted, hungry, weak from lack of food and unable to think rationally or make good decisions.

The truth was Serpent would have found her.

Miriam rung out the dishcloth and watched the water drop back into the sink. The thought of what would have happened made her feel as limp as the dishrag.

Thankfully, Abram had given her shelter and refuge. He had saved her life and kept her safe.

Emma returned from outside and shook her head. "My brother is far too impatient today. He stayed awake keeping watch through the night. He is tired and worried for our safety as we go to town." She scurried to retrieve more baked goods from the pantry as Miriam bowed her head.

"Thank you, Lord. You brought me to Abram. I'm sorry for the upset I've caused in his life, but I'm grateful he saved me. Keep all of us safe, Lord, especially today."

The kitchen door opened and Abram stepped inside and wiped his feet on the rug. His gaze went to Miriam with question. "You are all right?"

"I was saying a prayer for our safety today and giving thanks that you saved my life."

"I did not save you, Miriam. You saved yourself."

Abram was grateful for the clear sky and cool morning air as they rode to Willkommen. Emma was next to him, Miriam sat far in the rear, hidden from sight. She wore a white *kapp* covered with a black bonnet that pulled around her oval face and a cape that she held tightly around her neck. Thanks to the Amish clothing, even Serpent would be hard-pressed to recognize her if they came face-to-face.

The ride took longer than usual. Or perhaps it seemed long because of his anxiety about being out in the open, with no protection, when a man sought to do Miriam harm.

The tension he was feeling eased a bit when the town appeared in the distance. He flicked the reins and Nellie picked up speed, enjoying the exercise.

"A good horse provides for a man, just like a good wife," his father had said, but his father had embraced the old ways and never bent, even ever so slightly. After the accident had injured Emma's leg, he had not allowed the *Englisch* doctor to set her foot, leaving Emma with a decided limp and a constant reminder to Abram of his own carelessness.

The accident had happened when he was fourteen years old and he had carried the burden of guilt ever since. If only he had learned from his mistakes, yet he had remained stubborn when Rebecca's time of confinement had come to completion. Why had he not taken her to the *Englisch* hospital with her first labor pains?

"Is something wrong?" Miriam asked as if she could sense his internal struggle. The woman was amazingly astute and attuned to the way Abram responded to the world. His world. The Amish world.

"Nothing is wrong," he assured her. Except Miriam

was in danger and Abram feared for her safety. "We will be at the market soon."

Blocks of small shops and diners welcomed them to Willkommen. People hurried along the sidewalks and cars zipped past them on the road. Abram pulled on the reins for Nellie to halt at the first intersection. As soon as the light turned green, he flicked his gaze right then left, checking for traffic, before he nudged Nellie forward. The mare entered the intersection.

From out of nowhere a car, approaching from the intersecting roadway on the left, ran the red light and headed straight toward them. Abram's heart slammed into his chest. Emma screamed. He pulled back sharply on the reins as the car sped past.

"We could have been killed," Emma gasped as she stared after the fast-moving vehicle.

"The driver—" Miriam's voice was tight with emotion. "Did you see him?"

Abram shook his head. "I saw only the flash as the car passed too close to Nellie."

"He had crazed eyes and a sneer on his face," Emma said. "It seemed as if he sped up as he entered the intersection. His eyes were on the road as he raced through the light. I do not believe he even saw the buggy."

"*Gott* kept us safe," Abram said to calm the fear he heard in his sister's voice. But Emma was right. The driver had increased his speed.

"I saw his face." Miriam's voice was cold as ice.

A chill tingled Abram's neck and tangled down his spine.

Her next statement came as a whisper filled with warning. "The man driving the car was Serpent."

SIXTEEN

Miriam couldn't calm her racing heart even as she helped Emma and Abram unload the baked goods and crafts. They quickly set up a table at the side of the large hall, near a partitioned alcove where Miriam could hide if Serpent or anyone else involved with the Petersville police stepped inside. Abram and Emma seemed as aware of the danger as Miriam did. They hovered close and kept their eyes on the main door where shoppers, mainly *Englisch* ladies, started to appear.

Once the baked goods were arranged, Miriam turned to Abram. "I need to use a computer to contact my sister," she reminded him.

"After I find out if Samuel has returned to town."

Abram headed to the back door that led to the street where the buggy was parked. Through the open doorway, she watched him unload the handcrafted items he had made in his shop and carry them to the stall. Abram's fine craftsmanship and attention to detail easily made his woodworking stand out from other similar items Miriam noticed for sale.

"You could open your own store," she said as she placed his woodcrafts next to Emma's pies.

He grumbled.

"You should take pride in your ability, Abram."

"Pride is not from *Gott*. He gives gifts. It has nothing to do with me."

"But you use those gifts to give Him glory. Your wood-working ability is amazing."

"Your words puff me up too much, Miriam."

"Humility is knowing from where your giftedness comes," she countered.

Seemingly ignoring her words, Abram glanced around the marketplace then touched her arm. "Stay here with Emma. I will see if the sheriff has returned. His office is two blocks away, at the end of the alleyway in the rear of the market."

"Find out if anyone has seen a young blond woman with a thin, red-haired man. Also don't forget my aunt. Inquire about Annie Miller."

"I will ask at the sheriff's office and at some of the other stores around the square."

She grabbed his hand. "Thank you."

His gaze narrowed. "Serpent's focus was on the road when he passed us at the intersection. He did not notice who was in the buggy, but you need to be careful. The road he was on eventually leads to Petersville. Perhaps he has left Willkommen, but we cannot know for sure. You must be vigilant. The Amish clothing provides some cover but—"

"I'll stay out of sight," she quickly assured him.

With a nod Abram turned and strode out the back door of the market. Staring through the open doorway, she watched him for a long moment, expecting Abram to glance back and raise his hand in a wave or to at least offer her a smile of reassurance.

Instead he turned the corner and disappeared from sight. She wrung her hands and stepped into the shad-

owed alcove, knowing all too well that Abram was im-
mersed in a world that didn't include her.

Breathing out a deep sigh of regret, she peered from
her hiding spot to see a full-figured Amish woman approach Emma.

"What is it with your *bruder*?" the woman asked. "I had
hoped my daughter, Abagail, would catch his eye, but he
does not seem interested in finding a wife."

"Eva Keim." Emma straightened her shoulders. "You
know I cannot speak for Abram."

"No, but perhaps you could invite Abagail to visit."

"I will think on this," Emma said diplomatically.

"She would make a good wife for your *bruder*."

"I'm sure she would."

When the woman returned to her own stall, Emma
slipped behind the alcove. "I am worried about Isaac.
Usually he has arrived at the market by this time of day."

"Perhaps Daniel has delayed him," Miriam offered.

Through the open rear doorway and, as if on cue, Miriam saw a buggy pull to a stop. Daniel jumped to the side-
walk and ran inside. He quickly found Emma, who had
moved out of the shadows.

"Why are you running so fast, Daniel?" she asked. "You
look upset."

"*Yah*, a car passed us too quickly on the road. It nearly
ran us into a ditch. I was frightened."

Emma laid her hand reassuringly on the boy's shoulder.
"Who was it that caused you such fright?"

"I think it was the man who ran after me yesterday." The
boy pointed to his neck. "He wore a scarf and he screamed
at us as he passed by."

Emma hugged the boy and turned her gaze to Miriam.

Her stomach roiled. She had no right holding back information that allowed the killer to roam free. She had to

tell the sheriff as soon as possible about everything that had happened. Serpent had to be stopped before he hurt someone else.

Not Daniel. *Dear God, don't let anything happen to the sweet child or to his father or to Emma.*

Or Abram.

Her mother had been killed and her younger sister taken. How would she find the strength to go on if something happened to Abram?

"Keep him safe, Lord," she prayed aloud. "Keep them all safe."

SEVENTEEN

Upon entering the market, Isaac had confirmed the scare with the black sedan and his own concern for his son's safety. Now he and Emma were talking in hushed whispers so as not to let Daniel hear what they were saying. They were probably worried for the safety of both the Beiler and Zook households since Miriam had brought a killer into their midst.

She regretted her hesitation in notifying the authorities. Surely, Samuel Kurtz was back in town by now. Abram trusted him. She needed to, as well.

Needing to rectify her mistake, Miriam pulled the bonnet even closer to her face and the cape around her shoulders, and slipped out the back door, following the route Abram had taken to the end of the block. There she turned left and continued along the alleyway that led toward the center of town. Approaching the end of the second block, she spied the sheriff's office directly across the street.

Gathering her courage, Miriam headed to the corner crosswalk, but what she saw stopped her in midstep.

Her heart ricocheted in her chest. The sheriff had exited his office and was deep in conversation with another man in law enforcement. Miriam didn't need to see the man's face to know who he was. She recognized the scarf around his neck.

The sheriff was talking to Serpent.

She turned, needing to distance herself from both men. Seeing the sheriff so actively engaged with her hateful captor meant Samuel might be corrupt, as well. Did the sheriff know about the cabin and the way Serpent and his accomplice hunted women on the mountain road?

Memory of that fateful hijacking flooded over her again. Tears filled her eyes. She wiped her hands across her cheeks and tripped over her skirt as she turned to flee.

A man stood in the alleyway, blocking her escape. She flicked her gaze down the street. Where could she go?

"Hey, lady. Is something wrong?" the man said as she ran past him.

He raised his voice. "Do you need help?"

She shook her head and lifted her hand, hoping he would understand her need to hurry away.

"Sheriff," the man called out. Was he an overzealous Good Samaritan or part of Serpent's ring of corruption?

Fear grabbed her throat and wouldn't let go. All she could do was run. Except she couldn't run fast enough. The sound of footfalls followed her. Was it the man in the alleyway or Serpent?

She turned left at the next corner then made a fast right down another alley. At the intersection of a side road, she turned left and then right again.

Although unable to catch her breath, she was afraid to stop, knowing at least one man, if not more, was chasing after her. As much as she wanted to collapse in fear, she had to keep moving forward.

I can do all things through Christ who strengthens me.

Miriam had learned the scripture when she'd attended church and Bible study in Tennessee. Too soon, she had turned away from the good people who had wanted to help her. Was it due to fear of their admonition after she told them about her nomadic life and her unstable mother?

Or was she still ashamed of her mother as she had been growing up? Ashamed of her inability to keep a job or to create a loving home or face life's adversities? Her mother always ran away, which was exactly what Miriam was doing now. She was running from Serpent and the man in the alley and from the sheriff who might be involved in the corruption.

She needed to run away from Abram, too, and head to Atlanta. But what if Hannah wouldn't accept her into her home? Her sister had left three years ago and she'd never looked back or called to inquire about their health or their well-being.

The terrible truth was that Hannah wasn't interested in Miriam or her life. She was focused on other things that didn't involve her younger sisters and a dysfunctional mother.

Tears streamed from Miriam's eyes. She turned another corner and screamed.

Standing in front of her was Serpent.

His beady eyes widened. "It was you all along dressed in those stupid Amish clothes." He lunged for her.

Pulse racing, she turned to flee. Her foot slipped on one of the uneven pavers. She lurched forward, catching herself in time.

He grabbed her bonnet and ripped it from her head.

"No!" She ran, forcing her legs to move faster.

He chased after her, all the while cursing and calling her vile names.

Nearing the street corner, she heard the *clip-clop* of a horse's hooves and hesitated for half a second.

Serpent caught up to her. He grabbed her cape. She

shrugged free and ran into the street, directly into the path of an oncoming rig.

The Amish driver screamed a warning, but she couldn't stop. Serpent was on her heels and she would rather be run over than be captured again.

Abram hurried back to the market, expecting to find Miriam. He peered into the alcove and around the various stalls, searching for the *Englisch* woman who looked Amish with her tresses pulled into a bun and the *kapp* tucked securely on her head.

She was slender and tall and moved with a grace he found fetching. As he peered at the various *plain* women arranging their wares and selling to the customers who happened through the large common area, he saw no one that came close to Miriam's poise or beauty.

Emma was chatting with Isaac. He touched Emma's arm and smiled, causing a tug at Abram's heart. Why had he not noticed before now how Isaac leaned close to his sister as they talked, his attention totally focused on her?

She seemed equally smitten by the Amish man who placed his arm on the support beam against which she leaned. If Abram did not know better, he would expect Isaac to pull Emma into his arms and kiss her on the spot.

As much as Abram wanted to walk away and give them time together, he needed to find Miriam. Clearing his throat to get their attention, he stepped closer.

Emma looked up, startled. She pushed away from the support beam and tugged at her apron. Isaac dropped his arm and took a step back.

"I'm sorry to interrupt," Abram said.

Emma shook her head. "There is nothing to interrupt." But her flushed cheeks and dropped gaze said otherwise.

"Where is Miriam?"

Emma glanced around the warehouse as if she only now realized Miriam was gone. "She went to the buggy to get more supplies." Emma turned to Isaac, her gaze beseeching him to share what he knew about their houseguest.

He peered into the vacant alcove. "It has been some time since I have seen her. At least fifteen or twenty minutes."

Abram was already heading to the back door. Various scenarios played through his mind and none of them was good.

Once outside, he raced to the buggy but found it empty except for a carton of homemade pies. Hurrying past the Amish men who were enjoying a bit of socialization while the womenfolk sold their wares, he peered into the next buggy and the one after. Fear grabbed his throat. He wanted to scream Miriam's name and raise his fist in frustration, neither of which would bring her back to him.

Abram started down the street, but seeing no one in the distance, he turned into the alleyway he had taken earlier. If Miriam was hoping to talk to the sheriff, she would have gone this way.

Please, Gott, let my concern be for naught. Surely she was close by. Perhaps she had grown tired and was curled in the rear of a buggy. He turned and glanced over his shoulder to make sure he had not skipped over one of the carriages, then, realizing he had checked each of them, he continued along the narrow alley. At the intersection he peered right and left. Shoppers ambled along the thoroughfare. Some carried bags of baked goods from the Amish market. Others held baskets filled with items they had purchased.

The faces became a blur. The one face he searched for eluded him. Where was Miriam? Had Serpent found her?

Abram's heart tripped in his chest. Sweat dampened

his brow and the back of his shirt, even though the day was cool.

At the next intersection he spied the sheriff's office. Earlier, Abram had stopped to inquire about his uncle. Ned Quigley had told him that Samuel had returned to town but was out of the office. Art Garner, the deputy injured in the vehicular accident on the road leading up Pine Lodge Mountain, remained on a respirator, unresponsive, with his wife at his bedside. The accident had occurred the morning after Miriam had appeared on Abram's porch and before he had realized the extent of the danger that surrounded her.

He hurried on to the next corner and studied the street. His gut knotted, his hands fisted and the thoughts that raced through his mind would have him confessing before the bishop if he acted them out.

Why had Miriam left the market? The woman was headstrong and determined to contact Hannah. Finding her aunt was another need. Abram had tried, but no one knew of an Annie Miller who had ever lived in Willkommen.

Hearing someone call his name, Abram turned to see Daniel running toward him. His blond hair blew in the wind. He clutched his wide-brimmed felt hat in his right hand and in the other hand he held something close to his chest.

"What do you have, Daniel? You're running faster than the wind."

"A bonnet and cape. I found them." The boy held them up for Abram to see. "Why would an Amish lady leave them on the street?"

"Where were they, Daniel?"

The boy placed the items in Abram's outstretched hand then pointed to the end of the next intersection. "At the corner by the traffic light."

Abram's stomach tightened. "You must go back to the market before your father starts to worry."

"But he said I could go into the alleyway and check on the horses," the boy insisted.

"Did he now?" Abram pointed him to the market. "You are farther than the horses. Hurry back, Daniel, and do not stop to talk to anyone. Stay with Emma and your father. I will return to the market soon."

The boy nodded and hurried along the alleyway. Abram watched until he turned a corner and disappeared.

Gripping the two clothing items, Abram hurried to the intersection Daniel had mentioned. He had to find Miriam. But looking up and down the street at the various shops, he wondered where she could have gone. Then an even darker thought filled his mind.

Had Serpent captured her again?

EIGHTEEN

Miriam huddled in the corner of a tiny church where she had found shelter. "Thank You, Lord, for the buggy that knocked Serpent to the pavement and allowed me to escape. Thank You, too, for this open church that provided a place to hide."

Looking up, she stared at the small cross hanging at the side of the altar. "Oh, Lord, I was wrong—so wrong—in coming to Georgia. Forgive me and protect my baby sister."

She dropped her head into her hands and cried.

"Miriam?"

Raising her head, she wiped her hands across her cheeks and turned to see Abram standing at the rear of the church. A ray of sunlight broke through one of the windows and washed him in light.

"I didn't know where you were." He hurried toward her and touched her shoulder. "Daniel found your bonnet and cape."

He placed both items next to her on the pew.

"Serpent chased after me. I barely got away. Then I saw the church." Miriam smiled weakly. "God provided a refuge."

Like the refuge of Abram's house.

He raised his thumb and dabbed at the tear still on her cheek. "We will talk to the sheriff."

She shook her head, adamant to stay clear of law enforcement and eager to tell Abram what she had learned about his uncle. "Serpent was talking to someone in front of the sheriff's office. An older man, receding hairline, thick glasses."

"That sounds like Samuel."

"That's what I feared. I refuse to talk to him, Abram."

"The two men aren't working together, Miriam. You can trust my uncle."

Could she?

She stared into Abram's eyes, willing him to understand her concern. Perhaps he wanted everything to end and felt the easiest way to be rid of her was to turn her over to his uncle.

"Did you find any information about my sister or my aunt?" she asked.

His eyes clouded. "No one knew of either woman."

"And my mother's family?"

He shrugged. "Miller is a common name."

Was Abram making excuses?

Miriam glanced again at the cross. *Oh, Lord, help me to see more clearly so I know what to do. Abram trusts his uncle, but I saw him with Serpent. If only Abram would understand my concern.*

"My mother couldn't have made up a town named Willkommen," Miriam said. "She was slipping into dementia, but she could remember things that happened years ago. It was the more recent events that eluded her."

"Perhaps her family lived deep in the mountains," Abram offered as explanation for not finding information about her kin. "Some folks keep to themselves and rarely come to town. Or they could have moved away long ago."

The explanation sounded plausible. Not that she felt any better about the situation. Miriam had come to Willkommen specifically to connect with her mother's family. Now, that seemed impossible.

"Stay here, Miriam. I will bring the buggy to the alley. I do not want you walking along the street where Serpent could see you."

She didn't want Abram to leave her, but he was right. She would be safer in the buggy.

He squeezed her hand. "I will not be long."

Her spirits sank as she watched him leave the church, knowing she would soon be heading to Atlanta, leaving Willkommen and leaving Abram. They were worlds apart, which broke her heart.

Abram parked the buggy in the alley behind the church. He tied the horse to a fence pole and turned his gaze up and down the narrow path, alert to any sign of Serpent. The back of the church was nestled in a cluster of oaks interspersed with magnolias. Their wide, waxy leaves provided thick cover from any passersby. At least, that was Abram's hope.

He hurried toward the church and double-timed it up the side stairway. After easing open the door, he slipped into the darkened interior. His heart stopped. The church was empty.

He glanced at the small cross, his heart hardening in his chest. *Don't take another woman from me, Gott.*

"Abram."

He turned, relief sweeping over him. Miriam sat huddled in a back pew.

"I heard someone open the door to the church. Then the person turned and walked away. I feared someone had spotted me and was notifying the sheriff."

Abram hurried to reassure her. "I told you Samuel can be trusted."

She shook her head. "I can't trust anyone, Abram."

"You can trust me."

Miriam stared at him as if weighing his words.

Even now she did not believe he would take care of her. Abram knew it to be true.

He pointed to the side door. "We will go out this way. The buggy is directly behind the church."

Together they hurried outside. Abram helped her climb into the rear of the buggy. Once she was settled, he encouraged Nellie forward. Rounding the corner of the church, Abram searched for any hint of danger.

"The market is not far. We will be there soon."

Miriam let out a deep breath. The sound carried with it an increased amount of frustration and fear. No matter how much Abram tried to reassure her, Miriam was in danger. She knew it. So did he.

NINETEEN

Abram turned the buggy onto the market road and pulled to the rear of the complex. "Wait here, until I will make certain Serpent is not inside."

He studied the street then stepped into the market complex and again searched the people who milled around the various stalls. Thankfully he saw only local women buying produce and hand-crafted items. A few men chatted with friends. A few more sipped coffee purchased at a shop across the street.

Returning to the buggy, he offered Miriam his hand and helped her down. "This way." He quickly ushered her inside and then pointed her toward an enclosed office. "You can wait in here."

The office had a small leather couch and two straight chairs, in addition to a desk with a computer. Miriam sat on one of the straight chairs.

"Do I have to stay here for the rest of the day?"

"You will not have long to wait. Plus, you can use the computer. The office manager has a meeting across town, but I am sure he would not mind."

"What about the password?"

"Type in 'amishmarket.' All lowercase and no space."

She looked surprised. "You're sure?"

He nodded. "Remember, the Amish can use computers for business purposes."

"But you don't."

"That is right. Still, I know the password." He smiled. "You can trust me, Miriam, even if you do not trust all men."

She sat straighter in the chair and looked somewhat indignant. "What do you mean by that?"

"Your mother's actions made you wary of others, especially men. Did your mother make poor choices about those she invited into her heart? Or did she give the various men in her life more attention than she gave to you and your sisters?"

Miriam's expression told him he was right. He took a step closer and lowered his voice, hoping she heard the sincerity in his tone. "I am not like the men your mother attracted or the other *Englisch* men who caused you pain. You think I am uneducated or a fool or someone who does not understand the ways of your world. You look at the surface and do not look deeper. That is too bad."

"Abram, I'm—"

"You are sorry?" he volunteered. "Are you sorry because you cannot see me clearly? I hope you will heal from the scars you carry from your youth, and I do not mean visible scars. I mean the scars that bind your heart."

He turned and reached for the door. "I will return soon."

Abram found Isaac talking to Emma. "Miriam is in the office. Keep watch. I do not want Serpent to find her."

"You are leaving?" Isaac asked.

"For a short while."

Emma stepped closer. "I told you, you should not get involved."

"I already am. Keep Miriam safe."

"What will happen if she leaves you, my brother?"

He shrugged, unable to verbalize his feelings. "You have mourned long enough for Rebecca," Emma reminded him. "If Miriam leaves, you will mourn her, as well. I do not think she will open her heart to our faith and our Amish ways unless you ask her to do so. But I know you, Abram. You are a proud man. Too proud to ask her to stay."

"Then we will say goodbye," he said, holding his emotions in check. "And she will leave me."

His heart would break, he failed to add.

Miriam couldn't stop thinking of Abram's accusations. Had her mother and the string of self-absorbed men to whom she had been attracted turned her daughters against all men?

Miriam dropped her head in her hands, realizing how her own heart had hardened over time. Abram was right. Her opinion of men was a product of her nomadic youth and the stream of men her mother had allowed into her life.

Miriam didn't trust men. She didn't trust herself, either. She was her mother's child. Surely she was prone to make mistakes just as her mother had done so many times.

And Abram? Could she trust him with her heart? That was the question she kept asking.

Needing to contact Hannah, she scooted her chair to the desk, used the password Abram had provided and accessed her email. Quickly she composed a message to her sister.

Hannah, email back and let me know your phone number. We need to talk. So much has happened.

She briefly explained the hijacking, their mother's death and Sarah's disappearance, and that she had been holed up on the Zook farm in Willkommen.

I'm planning to take a bus to Atlanta and need you to pick me up at the bus station.

Miriam hit Send just as a knock sounded at the door. Emma peered into the room. She smiled at Miriam and stepped inside.

"Abram was worried. I'm glad he found you."

Miriam explained what had happened. "I hid in a church, never thinking anyone would look for me there."

"But Abram did."

"Thanks to Daniel finding the bonnet and cape. He's a good boy, and his father is a good man. You deserve a life of your own, Emma. You don't need to care for Abram."

"I was worried about him after Rebecca died. Things have changed and so has my brother. You have made him think beyond his grief and have given him hope for the future."

"You're wrong," Miriam insisted. "I've brought only problems to his life. No matter what you say, I have to leave. Abram said the bus to Atlanta runs later in the week."

"The bus runs at 10:00 a.m. tomorrow and the next."

"You took the bus to Ethridge when you went home to visit your parents?"

"Yah?"

"Did Abram drive you to the bus station?"

"I took the Amish Taxi. Frank Evans makes his living transporting the Amish." Emma glanced at the business cards taped to one corner of the small desk. "See, here is his information. People often use the office computer to contact him."

"The taxi is allowed?"

"We cannot drive, but we can ride in vehicles. It is confusing to one who is not Amish." Emma scowled. "But you cannot leave now. When it is time, Abram will take you to the station."

Miriam sighed, knowing she had already stayed too long. "I just emailed my sister. Once I hear back from her, I'll head to Atlanta."

Emma wrinkled her brow. "But your sister left you, *yah*?"

Miriam nodded. "I can't blame Hannah. There were times when I wanted to leave, as well."

"Yet you did not leave. You are like me, Miriam. You are the one who cares for others. You stayed to care for your mother."

Emma took a step closer. "You told me to think of my own needs. You must do the same. You were a dutiful daughter, but now you must make your own way in life."

"I can't think of anything until Serpent is captured and my sister Sarah is found."

"And after that?" Emma's gaze was filled with question. "What will you do then?"

"I will try to heal my heart."

Emma touched Miriam's shoulder. "You must unchain your heart, Miriam. As I said, we are alike. We can see what we want but we hesitate to accept happiness into our lives. A woman should be with a man. It is the way of life. You are rejecting who you truly are and what is best for you."

"I'm not sure you understand who I am, Emma."

"Take time to think things through, Miriam. I need to return to the stall, but you must not be hasty in your decisions to leave Willkommen. Promise me, you will weigh your options."

Miriam appreciated the Amish woman's concern. "I promise."

When Emma left, Miriam tapped in the URL web site

for the Amish Taxi and scheduled a pick up at 9:00 a.m. the following morning. Then she checked her email inbox to see if Hannah had responded to her message. She found nothing from her sister, but she did receive confirmation from the Amish Taxi.

Just as she logged off, a noise sounded outside the door and Abram entered the cramped office.

Miriam's heart pounded when a second person stepped through the door. The man she had seen talking to Serpent. Sheriff Kurtz.

Abram had brought the sheriff to the Amish market without talking to her first. What Abram didn't realize was that he had exposed her whereabouts to a man who more than likely was part of the corruption. The sheriff had to be involved after the way he had been focused on Serpent.

Abram hadn't listened to her earlier concerns about his uncle. Instead, he had exposed her to someone working with Serpent.

What was Abram thinking?

Abram stepped to Miriam's side. "Samuel has come to help. He needs to hear your story."

The sheriff pulled up the other straight-backed chair and stuck out his hand to shake hers. He introduced himself and added, "I'm the Willkommen sheriff. Why don't you start by telling me what happened?"

Shrinking back in the chair, Miriam shook her head. "I saw you talking to a man outside your office. He has a serpent tattoo on his neck, only he covers it with a scarf."

"Pete Pearson." The sheriff nodded. "He stopped by to inquire about my deputy who was air-evacuated to Atlanta earlier this week. Pearson helps the Petersville police, but only in an auxiliary role. He aids with traffic and crowd control. He's not a bona fide law-enforcement officer. Abram said another man was with him the night you were stopped."

Miriam nodded but she failed to speak.

The sheriff hesitated a moment before adding, "You need to start at the beginning and tell me the whole story."

"Abram said I am wanted for the death of my mother." She glared at the sheriff. "Do you consider me a suspect?"

Samuel shook his head. "That came from the Petersville Police Department. From what Abram told me about the night you appeared on his doorstep, I in no way think you had any role in your mother's death. Tell me what happened, Miriam, so I can bring the guilty to justice."

She stared at him for a long moment and then haltingly began to recount the night of the hijacking.

Abram's heart went out to her as she shared the horrific details. Samuel had confirmed that the hijackers were not officers of the law. At least, Pearson wasn't. One man kidnapped and held women hostage, the other was a cold-blooded murderer. Both men were felons who needed to be brought to justice.

"My mother didn't understand what was happening," Miriam explained as she got deeper into the story. "Serpent told her to be quiet. She wouldn't calm down. When he grabbed my arm, she lunged at him, screaming."

Miriam dropped her head. Tears fell from her eyes. Abram rubbed her shoulder, hoping to convey his concern and understanding.

A box of tissues sat on a desk in the corner. The sheriff handed them to her. Miriam nodded her appreciation, grabbed a tissue and wiped her eyes. "I'm sorry. I still can't believe my mother's dead."

"What happened next?" the sheriff asked.

"When my mother grabbed my arm to pull me away from Serpent, the other man stepped from the police

car. He drew a weapon from his belt and shot her. I...
I screamed. Sarah sprang from the car. The other man
grabbed her."

"Can you describe him?"

"I wish I could. Serpent struck me and I must have
passed out. The next thing I remember was being held in
the cabin. I could hear water running nearby."

Miriam's eyes widened. "Serpent put us in two different rooms so we couldn't talk to each other. He tied me to
the bed." She glanced at Abram. "I...I presume he did the
same to my sister. I heard portions of phone conversations
and someone with a deep voice must have stopped by the
cabin at some point. He and Serpent talked about other
women. The deep voice mentioned Rosie Glick. I heard
them both mention 'trafficking.'"

"Rosie Glick was an Amish girl who disappeared about
seven months ago. Are you sure that's the name he mentioned?"

"I'm sure."

The sheriff made a note in a booklet he pulled from his
pocket and then nodded for her to continue.

"The night I escaped, a red-haired man came to the
cabin. I saw him through the window. He hauled Sarah
away. He said he'd take care of her."

Miriam put her hand over her mouth. "I think he
planned to kill my sister."

Abram continued to rub her shoulder, wishing he could
do more to offer support.

"Have you seen your sister since then?" the sheriff
asked.

"No, but this is the first time I've been in town. Sarah's
five-five with blond hair and big blue eyes. She's twenty-
one, slender, pretty and..."

Looking up with tear-laden eyes, she added, "You have

to find her. Serpent came after me today. You have to find him and the other man—the ringleader—and send them both to jail for murdering my mother. Find the red-haired man, too, but even more important, you have to find my sister."

The sheriff leaned closer. "Miriam, why didn't you come to me at the beginning?"

"Serpent said he would make it seem that I had killed my mother if I tried to get away, which is exactly what he did."

"Go on," Samuel prompted.

"After Sarah was taken, I knew I had to escape." Miriam continued to retell how she had managed to elude her captor.

When she finished, the sheriff closed his booklet and returned it to his pocket. "Abram told me you found his house."

She nodded.

He looked at his nephew with tired eyes. "But you didn't tell me about Miriam when I stopped at your farm the next day."

"I didn't know what had happened," Abram confessed. "Only later, after you were headed to the hospital in Atlanta, Miriam told me about the hijacking."

"I trust my men," the sheriff said, "But I can't blame you for not sharing the information with my deputies, especially when Miriam was a possible suspect in her mother's death."

Samuel offered Miriam a sympathetic smile. "I'm glad we finally were able to talk. Be assured I will do everything in my power to track Pete Pearson down and bring him to justice."

"He was in town earlier," Abram reminded his uncle.

"I'll let my deputies know. He should be fairly easy to find."

"Miriam should stay in town," Abram suggested.

She narrowed her gaze. "What?"

"You'll be safer here if Pearson is on the loose."

"But—"

The sheriff pulled his cell from his pocket and tapped in a number. He pushed the phone to his ear. "Curtis, this is Samuel. We need to find Pete Pearson." The sheriff smiled. "That's good news. Have Ned bring him in to the station so I can interrogate him."

Samuel shoved his phone into his pocket. "One of my deputies is with Pearson now. He'll arrest him and haul him in for questioning."

He turned to Abram. "Take Miriam home with you and Emma. She'll be more comfortable there. Pearson will remain in jail. I can't see how a judge would set bail after what Miriam has told me."

Samuel stood and took Miriam's hand. "You go back to the farm with Abram. I'll need to get a written statement from you, but we'll do that later."

"We'll leave now," Abram said to Miriam as soon as the sheriff had left. "I'll see if Emma can ride home with Isaac."

After the arrangements were made, Abram helped Miriam to the buggy. Once she was comfortably tucked into the rear seat, he encouraged Nellie into a sprightly trot. He needed to get Miriam to his farm as quickly as possible.

As they rode through town, Miriam remained quiet. Too quiet.

"It will be over soon," Abram assured her.

"I didn't think the sheriff would believe me."

"I told you Samuel is to be trusted."

"I didn't ask him about my aunt."

"But I did. He does not know anyone by that name."

"Maybe it was all in my mother's mind."

"I am sorry you had to relive her death." He thought for a moment and then added, "When you talked about her, it sounded as if she was trying to protect you. She loved you, Miriam."

Miriam's silence tugged at Abram's heart. Verbalizing what had happened had taken a toll. She had to be exhausted and upset.

Hopefully after Serpent was captured she would be able to heal. But then what would happen? Would she go back to Tennessee or head to Atlanta?

Abram knew one thing for certain. She would not stay in Willkommen.

TWENTY

Miriam found comfort recalling how her mother had tried to protect her during the hijacking. In the confusion of the attack, she had focused on her mother's outrage that night instead of the protective nature of her attempt to stop Serpent. Maybe, as Abram had said, her mother had loved her, after all. The realization took her by surprise. For as long as she could remember, she had believed her mother had thought of her as a complication.

Now Miriam wondered if she had been too hard on her mother. A single mom with no consistent employment. She couldn't remember her mother taking food stamps or welfare, yet they'd had food and clothing. Thrift-shop purchases and beans and rice more days than she'd like to remember, but food and clothing nonetheless.

"Did you ever believe something and then find out you were totally wrong?" she asked Abram.

He remained silent for a long moment. A muscle in his neck twitched. She longed to see his face to read his expression. The back of his head with his hat pulled low provided no clue as to what he was thinking.

Once again she had been too forward and wished she could retract her question. Better to remain silent than to cause more problems. If only she could have boarded a bus today. But how could she find Hannah if she couldn't contact her by phone or email?

A sadness overwhelmed her and she hung her head.

Abram turned his head slightly. "You are crying again?" His words sounded like an accusation.

She bit her lip and shook her head. "I'm tired, that's all."

"You are worried about what will happen."

He was right but she refused to answer him. She had already said too much.

"And, yes," he continued, "I have believed wrongly and regretted my actions."

Was he talking about taking her into his house? She should have kept running that night and never stopped. But that would have been even more foolish when she'd needed a place of refuge.

"I'm sorry for disrupting your life, Abram." Especially since he had wanted to find lodging for her in Willkommen. Abram didn't want her underfoot. Not now. Not ever.

He shook his head. "You have brought new life to my house, Miriam. You are not a problem. I am the problem. I have held on too tightly to the past. You may have heard Emma say this. She is right. The old ways must sometimes change. The Amish who came to Willkommen did so with the intention of making new rules in which to grow as a community. I could not accept the changes so I have never fit in. It was not their outreach, but my stubborn pride."

"You have the right to follow the ways of the past."

"My wife died because of my unbending pride. I lost a child, as well. This is not easy to carry. Some would say it was *Gott*'s will, but I say it was my stubborn heart that had to be right about everything. That is the burden I carry."

"The church I attended in Tennessee talked about God's forgiveness. We have to be contrite and realize we have done wrong. We also have to desire to change our ways, but if we long to be a better person, the Lord is a forgiving Father."

"*Ach*! But, Miriam, *Gott* is not the problem. My earthly father is. He would never forgive me."

She didn't understand. "Why would your father be upset that you remained close to the way he raised you?"

"In my youth, I erred."

"When you were a boy? Could he not forgive a child for making a mistake?"

"I was headstrong and struggled against the rules he established. I did not want to plow the field and wanted instead to go into town to see my friends, *Englisch* boys, who pulled me into worldly ways. Because I was angry, I hurried the horses and plowed the field too fast. At the corner when I was making a turn, I did not hear Emma's voice. In her kindness, she was bringing me water since the day was hot. I had borrowed a small battery-operated radio from Trevor, my *Englisch* friend, and had the music playing, so I did not hear her call my name."

Abram swallowed hard. "The plow caught her leg. I never heard her screams. My father ran to gather her in his arms. He raised his fist in anger at me and said I was not worthy to be his son."

"Oh, Abram, he spoke in haste and he was worried about Emma."

"He never looked me in the eye again. He acted as if I did not exist."

"Did you ask his forgiveness?"

"I was confused and did more things to upset him. Trevor was older. He had a car. We rode to the lake, but the road was windy and we were going much too fast."

Emma had told her about the drowning, but Miriam knew Abram needed to recount the experience himself.

"At a sharp turn, the car skidded across the road and crashed into the water. I managed to get out."

"And your friend?"

"He was trapped. I tried to save him."

Miriam touched Abram's shoulder. "I'm sorry."

"That is why I left Ethridge after Rebecca and I were married. I needed to prove myself."

"And you proved yourself by adhering to the Old Order."

"That is right. I am the reason Emma limps, yet she came to live with me after Rebecca died, knowing I needed help. Emma's heart does not harbor resentment. She has forgiven me, but I cannot forgive myself."

"Have you asked your father's forgiveness?"

Abram shook his head. "It would not change the way he feels or acts toward me."

"And what of God? Have you asked His forgiveness?"

"He knows my heart."

"But acknowledging our wrongdoings and verbalizing our contrition aloud can be cathartic, Abram."

"Now you are sounding like the bishop." Abram shook his head. "*Gott* took Rebecca from me because of my willfulness as a young man. I did not deserve happiness after what I did to Emma and what happened at the lake."

"You're wrong, Abram. God didn't take Rebecca or your child because of the mistakes you made in your youth. Death is part of life. Sometimes we don't understand why it comes when it does, especially when the person is young and has their life ahead of them."

"What of you, Miriam? You spoke of your own actions and feelings that you have done wrong. Have you asked God's forgiveness?"

Abram was right. She hadn't sought forgiveness. She hadn't put the pieces together to see clearly the part she played in her own mother's wayward life.

"I never thought my mother loved me. Now I realize I might have been wrong."

"Can a mother ignore her child?"

"It seemed that mine had, but I was seeing life through my own childish eyes instead of taking into consideration her own struggle. I'm beginning to look at my youth in a new way."

For so long she had buried the pain of her past in the depths of her heart. Once free from Serpent, then and only then, would she work on forgiveness. By that time, she would have forgotten Abram.

Inwardly she scoffed at herself. Staring at the tall expanse of man as he held the reins lightly in his strong hands, she knew she'd never forget him. She would carry the memory of Abram in her heart for the rest of her life.

The Amish way of life and especially this righteous man who didn't see the good in who he was would remain forever a part of her. She would remember this special time, not because of Serpent and his wicked ways, but because of Abram.

Hopefully, his decision to notify the sheriff wouldn't cause her more duress. Too much had already happened. She didn't need any more trauma in her life. She needed peace and security, like what she had felt in Abram's arms. But that was in the past. And now Miriam needed to focus on the future.

Tires squealed and an engine whined as a vehicle left Willkommen and raced toward the buggy at breakneck speed. Abram clutched the reins more tightly and silently prayed for Nellie to remain calm, knowing anything could spook the horse when the car passed by.

Miriam leaned forward and grabbed Abram's arm. "What's happening?"

He peered around the corner of the buggy. His stomach soured, seeing the auxiliary police car with the portable flashing lights.

The car increased its speed even more and headed straight toward them.

"What is it, Abram?" she asked again.

The buggy jostled from side to side.

"Sit back and hold on," he warned.

"It's Serpent, isn't it?"

"I...I cannot be sure. He will soon pass us by."

Nellie fought against the bit. "Whoa there, girl," he soothed, trying to guide the mare to the side of the road.

The horse's ears twitched. Abram saw her flared nostrils and the whites of her eyes. "Quiet down, Nellie girl. Everything is okay."

Except everything was wrong. The Serpent was gaining on them. Yet he was supposed to have been taken into custody.

The engine of his car whined. The black sedan passed in a swirl of dust then screeched to a stop in the middle of the road.

Abram tugged on the reins, working to control the mare.

"I thought Ned Quigley was going to apprehend Serpent." Miriam's voice was tight with emotion.

"He must have gotten away."

"Or your uncle was lying."

"Get behind the seat, Miriam. Hide under the tarp."

"It's too late. He's knows I'm with you."

"He knows no such thing. Do as I say."

"But—"

"Now, before he steps from his car."

She scurried into the rear and dove under the tarp.

Abram climbed out of the buggy. "Nice girl," he soothed, rubbing Nellie's flank then her neck.

The mare was as confused as Abram. What had happened to Deputy Quigley and why was Serpent on the loose?

Abram narrowed his gaze as the driver's door of the black sedan opened. Serpent stepped to the pavement but left the motor running and the lights continuing to flash.

"You're leaving town in a hurry," the man growled.

Abram stood his ground. "Move your vehicle so I can pass."

"No way, Zook." Serpent stepped closer. "You've got something I need in your buggy."

"I know of nothing in my buggy that would interest you." He paused a moment and then pulled his lips into a strained smile. "Unless you want to buy an apple pie."

"Don't make jokes, Amish boy. I know Miriam Miller is with you."

Abram did not like Serpent's comment or his tone, and he certainly did not like being called an Amish boy. But his main concern was Miriam's safety. No matter what Serpent tried, Abram had to keep her safe.

"The sheriff wants to talk to you, Pearson."

"Sheriff Kurtz?" Serpent's eyes widened. "I saw him earlier today."

"He wants to talk to you about something that happened a few nights ago," Abram continued. "Deputy Quigley was supposed to have hauled you in for questioning about a car you stopped on the mountain road."

"You're talking crazy, Zook, as crazy as your Amish ways."

Abram refused to be intimidated. "You pretended to be law enforcement."

Serpent inflated his chest. "I *am* law enforcement, farm boy. I work for the Petersville Police Department."

"You work in a part-time auxiliary capacity. It is not the same."

"Since when does an Amish pacifist know anything about law enforcement?"

"I know legitimate officers of the law when I see them. I do not see such a man in you."

Pearson's face darkened. He fisted his hands. "Move aside, Zook. I don't want you to get hurt."

"You cannot hurt me, Pearson."

"Don't be so sure." Serpent tried to push past Abram and peer into the buggy.

"You do not have the right to encroach on my private property," Abram stated calmly.

"Encroach?" Pearson laughed. "Who taught you that ten-dollar word? Surely not the schoolmarm in your one-room schoolhouse."

The Serpent stretched his hand toward the tarp in the rear of the buggy. Abram grabbed his arm. Pearson turned and landed a punch to Abram's chin.

The blow stung, but Abram refused to respond.

Pearson tried to pull another punch. Abram ducked then grabbed Serpent and locked his arms in a tight hold behind his back. In one swift motion Abram removed the weapon from Pearson's belt.

Serpent struggled but Abram held him all the more tightly. Using his free hand, he removed the magazine from the gun and placed the unloaded weapon on the seat of his buggy.

"You'll pay for this, Zook."

"I have done nothing wrong. You are the one who harbors evil in your heart." Abram tugged on the end of the scarf, which dropped to the ground, exposing the tattoo as well as a cut on Pearson's neck.

"You wear the mark of the evil one. Change your ways,

Pearson, or you will regret your actions when you come to the end of your earthly journey."

The wail of a siren sounded in the distance.

Pearson glanced at the road, seeing the approaching car, and strained against Abram's hold even more. "You'll regret this, Zook. Chief Tucker will haul you into the Petersville Police Department and explain the rights you don't have. You *plain* folks think you're above the law."

Abram tightened his grip on Serpent, relieved to see the deputy's car screech to a stop. Ned Quigley threw open the driver's door and hurried to offer assistance.

"Sheriff Kurtz said you've had problems with this guy." Quigley slipped handcuffs over Pearson's wrists. "I'll take him in for questioning. We'll hold him for as long as possible. Kurtz will keep you updated."

"I thought you were with Pearson earlier."

Quigley looked perplexed. "Someone's given you wrong information."

Abram would let his uncle resolve the confusion. Right now, he wanted to leave Willkommen and all that had happened behind and return Miriam to the security of his farm.

He climbed into the buggy, and with a flick of the reins, Nellie started toward home. Once they were clear of the two vehicles, Miriam crawled out from under the tarp.

"Is it over?" she asked.

Abram nodded. "Serpent has been taken in for questioning. Hopefully he will stay in jail for a very long time."

Serpent's apprehension meant Miriam was no longer in danger. Nor did she need Abram's protection. While that should have brought relief, all Abram could think about was having to say goodbye to Miriam.

TWENTY-ONE

Miriam entered the farmhouse and hung the cape and bonnet Serpent had ripped off her on the peg by the door and shivered at the memory of rounding the corner and finding him on the street. Having him chase after their buggy when they were leaving Willkommen sent another shot of nervous anxiety to tangle down her spine. Thankfully Serpent had been apprehended, but even that did little to calm her troubled spirit.

The house was too quiet and she glanced around the kitchen, feeling totally alone. Emma was in town, and Abram was unhitching Nellie. Still shaking from the run-ins with Pearson, Miriam kept imagining what would have happened if Serpent had pulled back the tarp and found her in the buggy. Would Abram have held fast to his Amish nonviolence or would he have fought to protect her?

What did it matter? Abram was too enmeshed in the past. Not the adherence to the Old Order Amish ways—she understood that—but to his life with Rebecca. He couldn't get over her death and would carry the guilt that was ill-founded for the rest of his life.

Such a shame that he couldn't forgive himself.

He had asked her about her past. Had she forgiven her mother?

Miriam glanced around the large kitchen with the finely crafted table and benches and the sideboard where Emma cooled her pies. A clock and calendar hung on the wall. Two oil lamps sat on shelves with tin plates behind them to expand the arc of light when night fell. Everything about the kitchen warmed her heart with a sense of home, the stable home Miriam had never known.

As much as Miriam wanted to climb the stairs and hole up in her bedroom so she wouldn't have to see Abram again, she couldn't run away. Emma would be late coming home and the burden of preparing the meal always fell on her shoulders. Surely, Miriam could prove herself useful instead of being a burden. That's what she'd heard her mother say once about her daughters—that they were a burden. The word still cut a hole in Miriam's heart. How could any mother say that about her child?

Hot tears burned her eyes but Miriam refused to cry. She wouldn't let her face be splotched and red when Abram came indoors. She didn't need his perusal or questioning gaze. She had already said too much to him and had allowed herself to be too taken in by him. She'd learned her lesson.

Love and a happy home weren't for her, especially not with an Amish man who longed for his dead wife. Miriam could never compete, not that she wanted to. If Abram didn't accept her for who she was, then he wasn't the man for her.

She would find someone else.

Or would she?

In reality she knew she wouldn't. She would go through life with the wall around her heart, the way she had lived for the past twenty-four years. Abram had broken through that protective barrier for the briefest of times. She had made a mistake letting him in. A very big mistake.

* * *

Abram dallied in the barn, biding his time. He wasn't ready to face Miriam again. The run-in with Serpent had unsettled him. The man had held Miriam captive and hurt her and had come so close to finding her again.

Perhaps Abram had been too quick to bring his uncle into the situation. Had the meeting at the Amish market led to Serpent learning Miriam's whereabouts? Abram needed to return to the market tomorrow and would talk to his uncle then. Samuel would be able to clarify some of the confusion as well as provide information about how long Serpent would be held in custody.

Although relieved that Serpent had been apprehended, Abram was still troubled about another issue. His sister's earlier admonition continued to swirl through his mind. Emma was right. Abram was prideful. He was also fearful of what Miriam would say if he asked her to stay, to join the Amish faith and give their future a chance. He had lost a love once. He was not willing to open himself to that pain again.

Eventually, Abram ran out of chores that needed to be done. He was weary, not so much from physical exertion but more from a heaviness of heart that weighed down his shoulders.

Tonight he would talk to Miriam once Emma retired to her room. He would ask forgiveness for surprising her with his uncle's visit to the market. He did not want to do anything to hurt her or to cause her harm. He would never be able to forgive himself if he caused her pain. If she readily accepted his apology, perhaps he would find the wherewithal to broach the subject of their future.

Hoping their differences could be resolved and feeling a swell of optimism, he opened the door to the kitchen.

Emma had come home and was standing at the stove stirring a pot of soup.

He stepped inside and wiped his feet on the doormat, inhaling the pungent smell of onions and peppers and tomatoes.

"I did not see you come home," he said to Emma.

"Isaac walked me to the front door so we could talk a few minutes before I entered the house."

Abram glanced into the main room. "I do not see Miriam."

"She was so thoughtful and prepared a vegetable soup with some of my homemade noodles. I was relieved when I came in and smelled the wonderful aroma filling the house."

"Where is she?"

Emma's face grew serious. "She's upstairs, Abram. She said she's tired and wants to get some rest."

He glanced at the stairwell. "Surely she will eat with us."

Emma shook her head. "Not tonight. She's not hungry."

"What else did she tell you, Emma?"

"Only that she plans to take the bus to Atlanta."

"When?"

"I cannot say. All I know is that she emailed her sister today." Emma's face softened. She touched his arm as if offering support. "Abram, there is no reason for her to stay here."

"Serpent has been taken into custody. The sheriff needs a statement from her. And what of the trial? She will have to testify."

"Then she can return. But trials take time. It might be months from now. She must move on with her life."

Emma pointed to the table. "Come and sit, Abram. I will get your soup."

He shook his head and turned toward the door. "I have work to do in my workshop."

"You must eat."

"I am not hungry." Pulling his hat from the hook, he opened the door and stomped into the cold night.

Halfway to the workshop, he stopped and looked at the window of the room where Miriam was staying, hoping he would see her standing at the window. The room was dark and the only thing he saw in the glass was the reflection of the night sky.

His heart felt equally dark. He had tried to give of himself, but he had not given enough. In his youth, he had injured Emma. Trevor's accident had followed soon after. Three years ago he had lost his wife and child. Now he was losing Miriam.

His shoulders slumped as he entered the workshop. Miriam was already focused on Atlanta and the life she would live there. She would say goodbye to Willkommen. She would say goodbye to Abram, as well.

TWENTY-TWO

Miriam's mood the next morning was as overcast as the sky, knowing this would be her last few hours in the North Georgia mountains. At 10:00 a.m. she would board the bus to Atlanta. She would return for Serpent's trial, but she would find a place to stay in Willkommen or perhaps even drive up from Atlanta for the day she gave her testimony. Abram would remain on his farm and never know that she had returned to town.

His bedroom door opened and his footsteps sounded in the hallway. He paused outside her door. If only he would knock and ask her to stay or at least offer her some hope that she might have a place in his faith and in his future.

She bit her lip and hung her head, hearing him hurry down the stairs where Emma was, no doubt, preparing breakfast. They had more wares to sell at market today. Miriam would not interfere with their work and their routine. Plus, saying goodbye to Abram would be too painful. She hadn't even told him she was leaving. Another mistake on her part, but she didn't have the courage or the strength to face him this morning.

She had arranged for the driver to pick her up at nine, in time for the ten o'clock bus to Atlanta. She would leave a note of thanks for Abram's hospitality and Emma's friendship. She was grateful and so very thankful that she had found them.

Gott had provided, as they would say, and Miriam was beginning to see God working in her own life. The teachings that had started when she'd visited the church in Tennessee were put into action here on this Amish farm. She saw the hand of God in Abram and Emma's love of nature and closeness to the land, in their dependence on God's mercy for all things and in their rejection of the world that had gone too far off course.

For so long Miriam had yearned for a simple life where God was the center of the family and all was done to give Him honor. She'd found that here with Abram.

A door slammed below. She neared the window and peered into the morning stillness. Abram came into view, his shoulders back, head held high and his steps determined as he walked to the barn. She took a step back in case he looked up to catch a glimpse of her.

Today his focus was on the barn and hitching Nellie to the buggy. A knife cut deep into her heart. She had hoped he would change, but he wouldn't. He never would. Abram was...well, he was Abram, a strong man with a stubborn streak that could be a blessing or a curse.

A tap sounded at the bedroom door. Miriam hadn't heard Emma's footsteps on the stairway, but she was grateful the Amish woman had come to see her.

Pulling open the door, Miriam almost cried, knowing this would be the last time she would see the sweet face of the woman who had found a place in her heart.

"We are going to town," Emma said, her voice low as if to keep Abram from hearing. "Come with us, Miriam."

"Did Abram want you to talk to me?"

She could see the truth in Emma's eyes. The woman

would not tell a lie, but she couldn't admit that her brother had not mentioned Miriam. Had he even thought of her?

"I know he wants you to join us," Emma pleaded. Yet Miriam knew that what Emma believed and what Abram wanted were two very different things.

"You go, Emma. I need to finish my crocheting." The scarf she was making for Emma. "And cut the fabric for the dress you showed me how to make. I'll stay busy while you sell the rest of your wonderful items."

"Isaac will be working at the dairy for a few more hours, if you need anything. I could stop by his house before heading to town and ask Daniel to visit you. He's good company."

Miriam smiled at Emma's thoughtfulness. "Daniel is so special, but I'll be fine. Have him stay with Isaac."

"If you are sure."

Miriam nodded. "I am." She hesitated and then broached the subject she had already discussed with Emma too many times. "Isaac cares deeply for you. I see it in his eyes, and Daniel beams when you are near. He needs a mother. Isaac needs a wife."

Emma's cheeks blushed. She lowered her eyes momentarily and, when she raised her gaze again, Miriam could see the internal struggle that tore at the sweet Amish woman. "What am I to do about Abram? He, too, needs a wife."

"Your brother will not change until the situation becomes too dire. Right now you are enabling him to go on and not think about the future. He still longs for Rebecca."

"*Ach*, that was so true, but when you came into his life, Miriam, you made him think of what could be."

"He never showed signs of his change of heart to me. Do not lose your own happiness because of trying to help your brother. Isaac will not wait forever. Abram will understand. He talks about what a good woman you are, Emma, and he's right. But you must think of a little boy who needs you and a man who God has placed in your path. You will help Abram if you force him to be on his own. Only then will he realize what he really needs."

"I shall talk to him today. When we return home this evening, I will let you know how he takes the news. You are right, Miriam. Abram is locked in the past. I must encourage him to think of tomorrow."

Tomorrow. The word saddened Miriam. Hannah would meet her at the bus station this afternoon, and by tomorrow, Miriam would be trying to start a new life for herself. After the peace of the Amish life, she wasn't ready to face the hectic pace of the city.

Miriam grabbed Emma's hand. "Pray for me. I, too, need clarity about the future."

Emma nodded. "I will pray for you and Abram. You both struggle with the past."

"What do you mean?"

"Your mother. You cannot see the truth about her heart. She loved you even if she could not express that love."

"I believe it with my head, Emma, but my heart still questions her love."

"My mother wanted Abram and Rebecca to remain in Ethridge, close to her. She wanted what every woman wants, grandchildren around her in her old age. I saw her heart break when Abram left. He was the favorite child, and after Rebecca's death, my mother encouraged me to move to Willkommen to help Abram. As concerned as she was about Abram's well-being, I knew she loved me, as well."

"But what about your father. He never forgave Abram."

"That is how Abram sees the past. In reality, Abram could never forgive our father for his words spoken in haste. Both men are cut from the same cloth. Abram waits for my father to show some sign of forgiveness and our father waits for Abram to ask the same. They will never reconcile until one of them swallows the pride that fills each of them too full."

Emma squeezed Miriam's hand one last time. "Pray for Abram. He needs your prayers and your love."

With a sad smile, Emma hurried down the stairs.

The sound of Nellie pulling the buggy to the edge of the porch drew Miriam back to the window. Her hand touched the cool glass as if she were reaching out to Abram one last time.

He took the basket Emma carried and placed it on the floor of the buggy as she climbed into the front seat. He flicked the reins, signaling for the mare to be on her way. The buggy creaked. Miriam kept her gaze on Abram until he and Emma disappeared from sight.

If only he had glanced back. But Abram didn't need her, he didn't want her. He had his Amish life and everything that entailed. It didn't include an *Englisch* woman who brought strife and danger to his peaceful home.

Miriam would leave today. She would leave the Amish way. She would leave Abram, and that broke her heart.

TWENTY-THREE

Miriam quickly dressed in her jeans and sweater, feeling strange in her old clothes that used to be so comfortable to wear. She stuck the wad of fifties she had retrieved from her car in her pocket and then finished crocheting the scarf and left it on the bed with a note for Emma. She had also crocheted a woolen scarf for Abram to wear when the winter came next year. He could wrap it around his neck when the days were cold and he worked outdoors.

She gazed though the window at the horses grazing on the hillside. Would he even remember her or what they had shared by then?

She wrote a second note, this one to Abram, but she kept it breezy and light. No reason to bare her soul at this late date.

With a heavy heart, she hurried downstairs and poured a cup of coffee. After cutting a slice of Emma's homemade bread, she covered it with apple jelly. She would never find breakfast as good in the city. She would never find a life as good as here on the farm.

Once she had eaten, she washed her cup in the sink and then glanced at the wall clock. The car would pick her up in an hour. Not enough time to start a new project. Perhaps she should offer a prayer of thanksgiving for

the people who had taken her in. She wasn't used to praying, but it seemed appropriate. She folded her hands and
bowed her head.

*Lord, You provided a light in the window and a place
of refuge in my time of need. Thank You for Abram and
Emma and for the love I found in this home. Thank You,
too, for their faith that has shown me the importance of
placing You at the center of my life. Forgive me the years
of abandonment when I didn't have time for You. Forgive
me for my unforgiving heart closed to my mother's love.
Forgive me for arguing with Hannah before she left home.
Lead me to Hannah so we can reconcile. Protect Sarah
wherever she might be. If only Serpent would reveal her
whereabouts.*

She trembled, thinking of sweet Sarah and of what she
could be experiencing.

*Lord, I can do nothing, but I place her in Your hands,
and I trust that You, oh, God, will honor my prayer and
keep her safe. Let me not grow despondent about what is
to come, but let me know that You walk with me into each
of my tomorrows. With Your help, I will not despair, but
I will find a new life even if it is without Abram. Send an
Amish woman into his life who will love him the way I do.*

Love him? The thought startled her.

She shook her head. It was time to admit her feelings.
She loved Abram.

If only he could have recognized her love.

She sat for a long moment reflecting on all that had
happened. Then realizing there was something more to
tell the Lord, she bowed her head again and prayed aloud.

"Lord, You know my heart, but I still need to confess my
sinfulness. I made the trip to Georgia to find my mother's
estranged sister, hoping she would accept Mother into her
home so the burden for my mother's care would be lifted

from my shoulders. I thought only of myself. Forgive me, Lord, for my selfishness in my mother's time of need."

She sighed. "And, Lord, I love the Amish way and long to join this community of believers and the faith they follow. If only it were possible."

A faint knock sounded at the door. Miriam checked her watch. The driver was early.

She opened the door to find Daniel standing wide-eyed with his right hand outstretched.

"Did Emma tell you to visit me?" she asked, appreciating the Amish woman's thoughtfulness.

He shook his head. "No, but *Datt* told me this belongs to you. I found it in the pasture."

He opened his hand and revealed Miriam's cell phone.

Hot tears of relief burned her eyes. The Lord had heard her prayer.

"Oh, Daniel, I am so glad you found my phone. Thank you."

"It was protected by a pile of rocks. *Datt* said it should still work even with the recent rain. He said you can use the electricity that runs to the dairy barn to charge your phone."

Some of her heaviness of heart lifted. She would be able to see if Hannah had answered her email. Once she retrieved the contact information, she could call Hannah since her sister's number was programmed into Miriam's phone.

"Let me get the charger." She pulled the apparatus from the plastic bag that held her few belongings and hurriedly walked with Daniel to his father's farm.

Isaac greeted her warmly and ushered her into the barn where he pointed to the electrical outlet. "I wanted Daniel to give the phone to you before we left for market. We can wait until after you have made your call, if you would like to go to town with us."

"Thank you, Isaac, but I'll stay here. You've been so helpful. I'm very grateful to you and Daniel."

Miriam plugged in the charger and connected it to her phone, feeling another swell of relief as the cell turned on. Hannah had not sent a reply email, but Miriam quickly accessed her contacts and memorized her sister's phone number. She never wanted to be without a way to contact Hannah again.

Sending up a prayer of thanksgiving, she tapped the number into the keypad and pulled the phone to her ear, expecting to hear Hannah's voice. But the call went to voice mail. Miriam's euphoria plummeted so much that she almost failed to speak when she heard the beep.

"Hannah," she finally gasped. "It's Miriam. I've been hiding out in Willkommen. It's in the North Georgia mountains. I found refuge with the Zooks, an Amish family. I'm catching a bus to Atlanta later today. Can you pick me up at the bus station downtown? I sent you an email, but I'm not sure if you got it."

She pushed the phone closer. "I'm sorry about our argument when you left. Oh, Hannah, Mama's dead. She was killed by a man who stopped our car on the mountain road. Sarah was taken and I don't know where she is. The police...they were involved...at least, most of them. I have so much to tell you. I'm begging your forgiveness for the hurtful words I said. And Mama—I'm sure she loved us even if she couldn't show that love."

The voice mail beeped again, indicating the end of the recording. Had Miriam told her sister enough? Tonight she would arrive in Atlanta and she would fill her in on everything else.

Miriam allowed her phone to partially charge before

she left the barn, latching the door behind her. Isaac and Daniel were on their way to town and, just as yesterday, Miriam felt very much alone.

She ran back to Abram's house and hurried up the drive, but when she turned the corner of the house, she came to an abrupt stop.

Serpent.

Her heart crashed out of her chest and her pulse raced. She started to run, but he was too fast and too strong. He grabbed her shoulder and threw her to the ground. The cell phone slipped from her fingers. She screamed and raised her hand to protect her face as his fist crashed against her forehead, hitting her in the same place he had hit her before.

She tried to roll away from him, away from the heinous tattoo, away from the man who would take her to his mountain cabin and kill her.

Serpent had found her again. The last thing she thought of before she slipped into darkness was Abram's handsome face that she would never see again.

TWENTY-FOUR

Abram helped Emma set up their stall at the Amish market and, after the morning rush of customers subsided, he hurried to the sheriff's office.

Curtis Idler sat at his desk and greeted Abram with a warm handshake. "I'm sure you're here to talk to Samuel. He's at city hall with the mayor. I expect him back shortly."

"I wanted to know how the questioning went with Pearson. Did he reveal anything you can share with me?"

Curtis's smile waned. "Ned Quigley questioned Pearson after bringing him in yesterday. We held him overnight, but this morning a police officer from Petersville provided an alibi. They had worked together the night Miriam said her car was hijacked."

"The officer must have mixed up the dates," Abram objected.

"Ned said Pearson's alibi is tight. We couldn't hold him after that."

The reality of what Curtis was saying struck Abram hard. His chest constricted and a roar filled his ears. He leaned over Curtis's desk. "Are you telling me that Pearson, the Serpent, has been released from jail?"

"That's it exactly, Abram. He walked out of here this morning. The sheriff planned to tell you after his meeting."

"Then Miriam is in danger."

Curtis held up his hand. "Pearson is not a killer, Abram. You've got that wrong."

"I am right about the Serpent." As much as Abram wanted to deflect his anger onto Curtis, Abram knew he was at fault for leaving Miriam alone.

He glanced at his uncle's desk. "Tell Samuel to meet me at the farm. I fear for Miriam's life. If anything happens to her—"

Unable to continue, Abram stormed out of the office and hurried to the market to find his sister.

"I'm going back to the house," he told Emma. "Miriam cannot stay alone at the farm with Serpent on the loose."

"Be careful, Abram. Isaac should arrive soon. I will go home with him. But get to Miriam and make sure she is safe. She cares deeply for you, Abram. Open up your eyes and see the truth. Things change, and you have to bend, my brother. Tell Miriam how you feel and start by inviting her to join our faith."

His sister's words hit Abram hard. Miriam cared for him. Was Emma speaking the truth?

He hurried to the buggy and headed out of town. Nellie responded to the flick of the reins and was soon trotting at a rapid clip, but not fast enough to suit Abram.

Pearson knew Miriam was staying at the farm. He could have been watching them this morning. Watching and waiting until Abram and Emma had left the house.

Would Miriam be there when he arrived?

A mile out of town Abram spied Isaac's buggy coming toward him. Little Daniel sat next to his dad.

Abram pulled Nellie to a stop and called across the roadway to Isaac. "Pearson was released from jail, and I am concerned for Miriam's safety. Did you see his car on the roadway?"

"We saw no sign of Serpent. Daniel found Miriam's phone. She was charging her cell in the dairy barn when we left our house. The only car that passed by was the Amish Taxi."

"Frank Evans's service?"

"*Yah*. He said Miriam had requested a ride."

A chill settled over Abram. The bus to Atlanta stopped in Willkommen today. "I must hurry. Emma is at the market. Would you bring her home? And find Samuel. Ask him to drive to the farm. I might need his help."

"*Yah*. Of course. Be careful, Abram."

But he did not respond to Isaac's warning. He was too worried about Miriam and whether he would find her gone.

The ride home never seemed so long. Abram's mind kept playing tricks on him with terrible thoughts of what Serpent would do if he found her.

Please, Gott, keep Miriam safe.

Rounding a bend in the road, Abram spied the Amish Taxi approaching. He flagged the vehicle down and called out to the man at the wheel.

Frank rolled down his window and waved to Abram. "I had a scheduled pickup at your house. Miriam Miller. But she wasn't there when I arrived. I pounded on both the front and back doors of your house and checked the barn and woodshop. No one appeared to be home."

"You saw no one?" Fear gripped Abram's throat.

"The house sat empty. At least, that's how it seemed."

"She wanted a ride to the bus station?"

Frank nodded. "That's right. She scheduled the pickup so she could catch the 10:00 a.m. bus to Atlanta."

Abram said nothing else. He flicked the reins and encouraged Nellie to go even faster. He had to get home, and this was one time he wished for faster transportation. Nellie was a faithful horse that had served the family well, but she was too slow. Everything inside him screamed to be with Miriam. He knew deep down that something was terribly wrong.

He continued to worry when he turned into the drive. He leaped from the buggy, climbed the porch stairs and hurried inside, shouting her name.

"Miriam, where are you?"

Taking the stairs two at a time he climbed to the second floor and pushed open the door to the guest room. A note sat on the dresser.

He reached for it, afraid of what he would find.

"Thank you for opening your home to me, Abram, and for your generous hospitality."

What? He had invited her into his family. It wasn't a matter of hospitality. It was more. Far more.

Note in hand, he raced to Emma's room and on to his own, but failed to find Miriam.

"You made me feel welcome," he continued to read. "I felt such peace and comfort in your home."

He wanted her to feel more than comfort. He wanted her to feel acceptance and, yes, even love.

He ran to the barn, pushed open the door to find Bear whining to get out. "What happened, boy? Did you see Miriam?"

The dog barked and wagged his tail, which provided Abram no clue as to what had happened. He ran to the woodshed and his workshop and the outbuildings. Frank said he had checked them all as well, but Abram needed to make sure Miriam was not in any of the locations.

He turned to stare at Isaac's dairy barn. Perhaps she was making another phone call. A surge of relief swept over Abram. He started to run, eager to find her and tell her how he really felt. He would beg her forgiveness for his lack of understanding, for calling in the sheriff and for all the things he had done to hurt her, especially for believing his uncle when Samuel said Serpent would be held behind bars. He had thought Miriam would be safe at the farm today, but he had been wrong. Dead wrong.

Running along the drive, he stopped short, spying something in the grass. Stooping, he reached for the shiny object. A cell phone.

He tapped the screen. A picture of Miriam with two other women, one a bit older and the other a young blond. Miriam's sisters. Daniel had found the phone and returned it to Miriam, yet she had dropped it.

Abram's ears roared. Miriam would never accidently drop her phone. It had been knocked from her hand in a struggle.

His head swirled. He felt sick and afraid. Anger swelled within him at his own stupidity.

He heard the whine of an engine before the sheriff's car came into view. Samuel pulled into the drive.

Abram opened the passenger door. "Miriam is gone. Serpent must have her. We need to find the cabin where he held her before."

"Get in."

Once Abram had climbed into the squad car, Samuel pulled onto the road, heading up the mountain. "Where's the cabin?"

"I do not know, but she mentioned hearing water."

"There's a cabin not far from the river where she abandoned her car," Samuel volunteered. "The Petersville police said they would search the place, but we need to check it out ourselves."

Samuel's hands were tight on the steering wheel. "We'll go without lights or siren. I don't want to warn Pearson we're on to him. Surprise is our best weapon."

But would it be enough?

The sheriff pushed his foot down on the accelerator as he grabbed his radio and contacted the dispatcher.

"Miriam Miller has been taken. Alert all deputies and first responders. Roads leading from the Zook farm need roadblocks. Issue a BOLO for Pete Pearson, auxiliary member of the Petersville Police Department. Contact the chief of police there and get him involved."

Trees and boulders flew past the window. All Abram could see was Miriam's face, twisted with fear, and Serpent standing over her, the vile tattoo wrapped around his neck, with a gun to her head.

"Hurry, Samuel," Abram said, uncertain as to the impact of a look-out bulletin with the local law enforcement. "We have to get to Miriam. We have to get to her in time."

Miriam awoke to a déjà vu experience, hearing water and smelling the musty cot on which Pearson had tied her. She pulled against the restraints, needing to free herself.

Over the pounding of her heart, she heard a one-sided conversation that indicated Pearson was on his cell.

"That's right. I've got her at the cabin."

A long pause. "He recognized me today and remembered the woman. He was planning to notify the sheriff. I had to kill him."

A lump formed in Miriam's throat. Was he talking about Abram? Had Pearson killed him?

"You killed her mother," Serpent continued.

Miriam turned her head to hear more clearly.

"Just because she was screaming and saying how much she loved her daughter." Serpent's voice was raised, his anger evident. "You're as guilty as I am."

The reality of what he had revealed washed over her. In the heat of the attack, she had blocked out her mother's words. Now, as she relived again the moment prior to her mother's death, they returned in a flash of recall and, although still unable see the shooter's face, she heard her mother's words of love spoken from the heart.

"I love you, Miriam!"

The open wound that had festered deep within Miriam for so long, the wound of being unwanted, of being unloved, knit together as surely as if the Divine Physician Himself had sutured the gaping hole closed.

She was loved. Tears stung her eyes, but she wouldn't give in to them. She had to free herself so she could know what had happened to Abram. And Emma. Was that dear woman hurt, as well?

Abram couldn't be dead. It couldn't be true. It had to be a lie.

TWENTY-FIVE

Abram felt like a caged grizzly bear when they found the cabin by the water's edge empty. He climbed back into the sheriff's squad car.

"Where to now?" Samuel asked, his voice as hard as steel and reflecting the way Abram felt.

"Ezra Jacobs's place. Jacobs said he saw a tall redhaired man that matched the description of a person Miriam had seen at the cabin. The old man's memory is not the best, but perhaps he will have remembered more about what happened."

Samuel accelerated. "Hold on," he told Abram as he pulled onto the mountain road, heading for the turnoff to Jacobs's cabin. He made the sharp turn onto the narrow, pitted roadway that led up the steep incline, sending gravel and dirt flying.

They braked to a stop in front of the cabin, leaped from the car and raced to the porch. The sheriff called Ezra's name and announced, "Sheriff's office," before he entered the small abode. What they found took Abram's breath.

The old man lay on the floor in a pool of blood. His faithful dog, Gus, whined at his side.

The sheriff knelt beside Ezra and felt for a pulse. He

looked up with heavy eyes and shook his head. "He's gone."

Pulling out his cell, he called Dispatch and requested backup. "We also need the coroner, a crime scene specialist and an ambulance to transport the body to the morgue."

A siren sounded, heading their way.

"Tell everyone to go silent," Samuel said to the dispatcher. Within seconds, the shrill wail died.

As Samuel pocketed his cell, a car charged up the gravel trail and braked in front of the cabin.

Deputy Curtis Idler climbed from behind the wheel and hurried to join Abram and the sheriff.

"What happened?" he asked before he looked down and saw the body. He let out a lungful of air and shook his head. "Looks like we've got a killer on the loose."

Not the story Curtis had given Abram earlier when the deputy had claimed Serpent was innocent of wrongdoing.

"Did you question Ned Quigley about releasing Pearson?" Abram demanded as he tried to control his anger.

Curtis held up a hand defensively. "I told you what Quigley said. Pearson's alibi was airtight."

"I'm beginning to think I hired the wrong guy," the sheriff said. "Do you know where Ned is now?"

Curtis shook his head. "I haven't seen him all day. His girlfriend called and said he had a stomach virus, but I'm not sure if we can trust her."

"Why not?"

"She worked with the Petersville Police Department as a file clerk some years back. If any of those cops are bad, she might be part of the group."

"I'll deal with Ned when we get back to town," the sheriff assured Curtis. "Right now, we have to find Miriam Miller. Pearson may have her. She was previously held in a cabin situated near running water."

"Water? You mean the river? What about the abandoned cabin on the other side of the roadway?"

Samuel nodded. "We've already checked it out."

Abram stepped onto the porch and rounded the cabin. Jacobs had spotted the red-haired man. Surely the old guy didn't travel far from home, which meant Red had been close by. At the rear of the cabin, Abram spied the continuation of a roadway that angled under an overhang of oaks and disappeared up the mountain into the thick forest.

He came back and told Samuel.

"Let's go." The sheriff and Abram took the lead with Curtis following in the second car. The path was steep and rough, but they soon came upon a waterfall. The running water Miriam had heard.

Getting out of his squad car, Curtis drew his gun and pointed to a thick patch of hardwoods and pines. "I'll check to the right. You two head to the left."

Samuel held up his hand. "Stay behind me, Abram. Or you can wait in the car."

"I am going with you."

Abram wanted to push quickly through the brush, but Samuel insisted they take it slow. "We have to use caution and cover. We don't want Pearson to see us first."

He was right, of course, but Abram kept thinking of Miriam being held against her will.

Let her be alive. Please, Gott. I beg forgiveness for all my transgressions. For my sinful past. Do not let my failings keep You from helping Miriam.

The sharp report of a gunshot sounded behind them. Samuel turned and ran, retracing his steps as he headed in the direction of the gunfire. Abram passed him, fearing the worst. It couldn't be Miriam.

"Get behind me," Samuel warned. But Abram refused to slow down. He needed to find Miriam.

Passing the area where they had parked the cars, they raced into the thick brush, following the path Curtis had taken. Not more than fifty feet into the thicket, they spied the cabin and Pearson's body on the front porch with a bullet in his chest. Just like Jacobs, the Serpent lay in a pool of his own blood.

Curtis knelt over him and touched his neck. "He had a weapon."

"Did you identify yourself as from the sheriff's office?" Samuel asked.

"Of course I did," Curtis insisted. "He wouldn't drop his weapon. I didn't have a choice."

"Miriam?" Frantic to find her, Abram started for the cabin.

Curtis stepped in front of him. "I'll go first. You don't know who's in there."

"I do not care. I need to find her."

The sheriff stared down at where Pearson lay. He pursed his lips and turned to glare at Curtis.

"What?" A muscle twitched under Curtis's eye.

"Pearson's gun is still in his holster."

"He had another weapon. It must have fallen into the bushes."

Samuel took a step toward the deputy. "Give me your gun, Curtis."

"What are you talking about? Pearson was a criminal. He kidnapped a woman. She's tied up inside."

"Have you seen her?" Samuel stepped closer, his voice low and menacing.

Abram inched closer, needing to get into the cabin.

"Stay where you are." Curtis aimed his gun at the sheriff but flicked his gaze to Abram.

"Calm down, Curtis. There will be an investigation,"

the sheriff said. "If you're telling the truth, you'll be exonerated."

"You always think you know best. I was in line for sheriff until you decided to run for office. I knew I didn't have a chance. People thought you were the honest candidate because of your Amish background. They don't know that you left your community because you couldn't follow the rules."

"Give me the gun, Curtis." The sheriff inched closer. Abram did the same.

"You'll never get away with this," Samuel warned.

"Of course I will," Curtis boasted. "I'll blame it all on Pearson. He was a loser. He wouldn't follow my lead. He made me kill that old woman. I didn't want to, but she started screaming. At least her daughter didn't see my face. Pearson and I had been a team, but he got pushy and shoved his weight around. The mother was protective of her daughter, saying how special she was and how much she loved her. It made me sick."

Curtis shook his head with disgust. "My mother left me in a motel until child services picked me up. I was stuck in that room for two days. How do you think that feels, Sam? Do you have any idea? You were raised in a loving family and you turned your back on them. I didn't have anyone to love me."

"I'm sorry for your childhood, Curtis." Samuel's voice was filled with understanding. He took a step closer then extended his hand as if willing Curtis to give him the weapon. "I'll get you help. Someone to talk to you. You didn't do anything wrong, Curtis. I understand why you're upset at your mother. Did you kill the woman because she reminded you of your mother?"

Curtis's expression revealed the sheriff had hit too close

to home. The deputy shook his head. "Shut up, Sam. Don't talk about my childhood."

"You were a good kid. Your mother loved you. Something unforeseen must have happened to her so she couldn't get back to you." Another step. "Now give me the weapon. You can trust me."

Sam lunged. Curtis fired. The sheriff gasped, clutched his side and fell to the ground.

Abram raced toward the deputy. A second shot winged his chest and knocked the air from his lungs. He tumbled to the porch then crawled up the steps. Abram's vision blurred and the cabin swirled around him. Time stood still for one long, painful moment, then...

Footsteps sounded. He looked up, seeing Miriam dragged from the cabin with her arms tied in front of her. Curtis yanked her down the steps and into the brush.

Abram stumbled toward Samuel and felt his neck for a pulse. He was breathing, but his pulse was erratic. Abram grabbed the sheriff's cell and pressed the prompt for the dispatcher.

"The sheriff...needs an ambulance," Abram said when the woman answered. He pulled in a deep breath and continued on. "The cabin...sits up the mountain behind Old Man Jacobs's place. Have the sheriff's office set up a roadblock at the fork in the road to town. Contact the Petersville police. Instruct them to block the mountain road that leads there, as well. Curtis Idler his taken a hostage and will be heading in one of those two directions."

Samuel struggled to speak after Abram disconnected. "Go...now. Take...keys."

"I'm not going to leave you," Abram insisted.

"You drive. You can. Remember... Trevor."

Trevor, the friend who had taught Abram to drive, who

had loaned him his radio, who had encouraged him to leave the Amish way of life.

"I...know..." Samuel gasped for air. "You were...be-hind...the wheel."

The day of the accident. The day Trevor had died.

After Emma's accident, Abram had gone joyriding with his friend. Trevor had let Abram drive. He'd been reckless, moving too fast on a windy lakeside road.

"Go..." Samuel insisted. "Now."

"The ambulance is on the way. Hang on."

Abram grabbed the keys from Samuel's pocket and ran toward the clearing. He climbed behind the wheel of the sheriff's squad car, remembering his youth and the times Trevor had let him drive.

He turned the key in the ignition and stepped on the accelerator. The car lurched forward. The radio squawked as the deputies called in their locations. They were still too far away to help.

Abram gripped the steering wheel, seeing Curtis in the distance. The deputy was driving much too fast along the winding mountain road. Abram was as well, but he could not let him get away with Miriam.

Isaac's dairy came into view. He saw his own farm in the distance. Just so Emma and Isaac and little Daniel were still at the market and not anywhere near Curtis. Sirens sounded in the distance, approaching on the road from town. Their roadblock would stop the deputy. At least that was Abram's hope.

The deputy's car approached the fork. Abram's heart stopped. Curtis took the road to the right, the road that passed Abram's house. The road that led to the bridge.

"No," Abram bellowed. "The bridge looked stable enough, but the wood was rotten and would buckle with any weight. Miriam would be hurled into the water.

Just like Trevor so long ago.

Abram pushed the car faster. His hat flew off, his hands were white-knuckled on the steering wheel. He screeched around the bend. In the distance he saw the deputy's car heading straight for the bridge. Abram laid on the horn, needing to warn him. Curtis had to stop.

Abram's heart jammed in his throat as the deputy's car sailed across the bridge. In a split second the wooden platform groaned then crumbled like a child's toy, toppling the squad car—along with Miriam—into the raging river below.

Accelerating even faster, Abram drove to the edge of the bridge, screeched to a stop and leaped from the car. He threw off his jacket, kicked out of his shoes and dove into the water.

The frigid cold took his breath. He beat the rapid current with strong strokes that took him to the middle of the river. The car was already partially submerged.

Diving down into the murky river, he grabbed the passenger door that hung open and felt inside, searching for Miriam. She was not in the car, neither was Curtis. A cracked windshield big enough for a body to hurl through paralyzed him for one long moment.

Gott help me.

He surfaced for air, grabbed a breath and then dove deep again, beneath the car that was slowly sinking.

Miriam's sweet face, her smile, her eyes…she was all he could think of.

Where was she?

He stretched his arms, thinking of Christ who had died on the cross. *Gott, do not let her die.*

His hand touched something. A piece of fabric. He pulled it close, feeling the softness of her flesh. He wrapped his arms around her waist and kicked to the surface.

Sheriffs' cars clustered at the edge of the road. Police from Petersville had already lowered a boat into the water.

"Here!" Abram shouted, kicking his legs and holding Miriam close with one arm while he raised the other overhead.

"There's Zook," an officer shouted. "He's got the woman."

The boat neared. Hands reached for Miriam and pulled her from the water.

"I am all right. Get her to safety," Abram insisted.

When he started to swim, he realized his folly. He could not move his left arm. An officer in a second boat pulled him to shore. "You're wounded, Abram. It's a wonder you could swim at all."

But he had. He had found Miriam and saved her.

Once on land he raced to where she lay, pale as death, on a stretcher. "How is she?" he asked the medic who was working on her.

The EMT shook his head. "We're taking her to the hospital."

"I must go with her," Abram insisted.

"You can't. We'll bring another ambulance. Looks like you need to be treated, as well."

Abram's heart broke as the EMTs lifted Miriam into the ambulance. Would he ever see her again or had *Gott* taken another woman from him? A woman he loved and wanted to cherish for the rest of his life?

Emma was right. He had lived too long in the past. He wanted a future with Miriam.

But would she survive?

TWENTY-SIX

Emma and Isaac met Abram at the hospital. They had brought fresh clothing that Abram changed into, grateful for their thoughtfulness, as well as a plastic bag containing Miriam's belongings and her cell phone.

"How is she?" Emma asked, her face drawn and filled with worry.

He shook his head. "The doctor is with her."

Emma touched his arm. "They said you saved her, Abram."

He nodded.

"But you are wounded yourself, my brother."

"The wound is not deep. It will heal." He glanced at Isaac and then back at his sister. "Where is Daniel?"

"Eva Keim and her daughter are with him," she reassured him. "And Samuel? Is there news?"

"In surgery." Abram's voice tightened. "If he survives, he will have a long recovery."

"Curtis Idler's body was found," Isaac shared, his eyes downcast. "He did not survive."

Abram nodded. "Curtis was working with Serpent and is the one who killed Miriam's mother."

"What of the newly hired deputy?"

"Ned Quigley is a good man and a trusted officer of the law."

The day passed slowly. Abram appreciated Emma and Isaac's support, but his total focus was on Miriam.

The intensive care rules allowed visitors to be with the patients for only short periods. Abram's gut wrenched each time he entered her room, seeing her hooked to machines that monitored her heart rate and blood pressure and other vital signs. An IV bag of medication hung by the side of her bed and dripped life-giving antibiotics into her vein. She had aspirated water and the doctor worried about pneumonia setting in.

Abram placed the bag containing her things on the stand by her bed and wondered how long it would be until she was alert enough to know it was there.

By late afternoon Isaac was growing fidgety and increasingly concerned about his dairy cows and their need to be milked.

"Go home," Abram encouraged. "Take Emma with you. I will use the Amish Taxi and return to the farm later. The horses need to be watered and fed. The other animals, as well."

"I can do the chores," Emma offered.

"I appreciate your help, Emma, but you cannot do all of them." He thought of his sister's difficulty in walking. "You have already done so much for me. Go with Isaac. He needs you."

"But—" She started to object.

Abram took her hand. "It is time for you to have a family of your own, Emma. You saved me after Rebecca's death, for which I will always be grateful. Now it is time for you to embrace your own life."

"Are you sure, Abram?"

"More than anything I want you to be happy. You forgave me, Emma, when I could not forgive myself. Now I must let go of the past." He turned to look through the glass window into Miriam's room. "Now I must focus on the future."

Emma squeezed his hand. "I am praying for you, Abram, and for Miriam." Turning, she wrapped her arm through Isaac's. Together they walked out of the intensive care unit.

Once again Abram entered Miriam's room. He drew a chair next to her bed and took her hand as he sat. Her hair was matted from the river and her slender face was ashen, but Abram had never seen a woman more beautiful or more courageous. She had been through so much.

The doctors said he had saved her in the nick of time. Although infection was a concern, they were more worried about the drugs Serpent had used to subdue her. If only she would open her eyes and respond.

Abram rubbed her hand and leaned closer to the bed.

"Miriam, I do not know if you can hear me. It is Abram. I was wrong about so many things, but I know one thing for certain. I love you with my whole heart. I need you. Come back to me."

The nurse allowed him to remain at Miriam's bedside far longer than the allotted visiting period, but later that evening she ushered him into the hallway. "Go home, Mr. Zook. I know you have a farm to tend. You can do nothing here. We expect her to sleep through the night and most of tomorrow. Come back in the afternoon. We'll know more then."

Abram's heart was heavy as he rode home in Frank Evans's taxi. Thankfully the driver did not chatter as he usually was prone to do. Perhaps he realized Abram needed time to think and pray.

Entering the house, Abram felt numb with confusion and worry. Emma was there to greet him, along with Isaac.

"How is she?" his sister asked as she poured a cup of coffee for Abram and set it on the table.

"The same. The nurse encouraged me to go home. I... I did not want to leave but...the farm."

Isaac stepped forward. "I took care of the animals. You do not need to worry."

But he was worried. He was worried about Miriam.

"As Emma mentioned at the hospital, Eva Keim and her daughter, Abagail, are keeping Daniel tonight," Isaac continued. "I will pick him up tomorrow after the cows are milked. I can take you to the hospital before I get Daniel."

Abram appreciated the offer.

"I have a plate for you to eat, Abram." Emma ushered him toward the table. "You must be hungry."

He could not eat. Not now. "I will eat tomorrow."

Abram dragged himself upstairs. The door to Miriam's room hung open. He looked in, remembering the night he had placed her on the bed with her blood-stained clothes and her bruised and scraped face.

His mind flashed back to the moments they had shared: walking along the pasture path, in the barn and workshop, and on the stairway when he had taken her into his arms.

His arms were empty now. Would he ever hold her again?

Entering his bedroom, he reached for his Bible, but he did not have the strength to open to the words of scripture. He merely clasped the well-read book to his heart.

Forgive me, Gott, for the mistakes I have made. I see more clearly now that I was the one at fault and not my datt. I could not save Trevor so long ago, but You helped me save Miriam. I can no longer look back, yet I know a future with Miriam will never be unless she comes into the Amish faith. Right now, I ask that You allow her to live. Even if she refuses my faith, I will never forget her and will never stop loving her from afar.

TWENTY-SEVEN

After a sleepless night Abram left his bed early to do the chores and get everything ready for his departure. He planned to stay at the hospital until Miriam was released. He would bring her home to recuperate here with him. With Emma's good cooking and with the threat of Serpent gone, Miriam would heal both physically and emotionally.

True to his word, Isaac picked Abram up at his house and carted him to the county hospital.

"Shall I return this evening?" Isaac asked.

Abram appreciated the offer but he shook his head. "I will stay at the hospital tonight. I do not want to leave Miriam again."

Isaac nodded. "Do not worry about the farm. I talked to Eva Keim's twin sons. They will help."

"You are a good neighbor, Isaac, and a good friend."

"We take care of each other, Abram. It is the Amish way."

The way of life Abram had always lived. Only once, in his turbulent youth, he had yearned for a more worldly life. Emma's accident and Trevor's death had brought him back to his Amish roots.

Gott had brought good from those two very tragic situations. Hopefully good would come from Miriam's ordeal, as well. Abram had found the woman he wanted to walk with through life. If only she felt the same.

But she was an *Englischer* and he was *plain*. The divide stood between them. Hopefully it would not prove too large to reconcile.

Renewed in hope, he hurried into the hospital and headed for Intensive Care. He stopped at the nurses' desk to speak to the kind woman wearing scrubs who had reached out to him yesterday.

"How is Miriam?" he asked.

The nurse's smile was bright, which filled him with relief. "She had an amazing recovery. The effects of whatever drugs her captor had given her wore off last night. We started her on oral antibiotics and were able to release her from Intensive Care this morning."

Abram lifted up a prayer of thanksgiving and then smiled back at the nurse, eager to see Miriam. "Could you tell me to which room you have moved her?"

The nurse's face clouded. "I'm sorry, Mr. Zook. She's gone."

His heart lurched. "What?"

"A reporter stopped by, asking questions."

"A newspaper reporter?"

The nurse nodded. "That's right. I think it worried her. Soon after that she checked herself out of the hospital against doctor's orders. We would have liked her to stay another twelve hours or so, but we couldn't keep her against her will. I thought she would have contacted you."

"Where did she go?"

"I'm not sure. Do you know a man named Frank?"

"*Yah*, he runs the Amish Taxi."

"He picked her up. Hopefully he can help you find her."

"May I use your phone?"

"Of course." She handed a phone to Abram and pointed

to a small desk and chair in the corner. "You'll have more privacy over there. Dial 8 to get an outside line."

Abram's hand was shaking as he plugged in the number for the taxi service. Frank answered on the first ring.

"Miriam Miller," Abram said. "Where did you take her today?"

"To the bus station. She caught the bus to Atlanta."

Abram's world shattered. He sat clutching the phone, unwilling to accept what he had just heard.

Miriam had left him.

He had given her safe refuge. He had also given her his heart. But it was too little too late.

Miriam did not want an Amish man. She did not want Abram. No matter how much he wanted her.

Eleven days later...

Miriam walked to the window of the hotel room and looked at the street below where cars hurried, rushing through the city, heading to their destination. She had been in Atlanta for almost two weeks and had not found Hannah nor heard from her in all that time. Her older sister seemed to have disappeared just as surely as Sarah had.

Perhaps Hannah had discarded her old cell for a newer model with a new number and then left the city for places unknown. If so, the two sisters might never reconnect. The realization brought a heavy weight to rest on Miriam's shoulders.

The neon sign for the bus station flashed in the distance and brought memories of the day she had arrived in Atlanta, expecting Hannah to meet her. Instead she had found only strangers in the station. Crestfallen, Miriam had made her way to the cheap hotel nearby where she had spent the night crying from loneliness and a confused heart.

How much she yearned for the life she had found in the North Georgia mountains. In her mind's eye, she saw Abram's handsome face and felt his strong arms surround her as he lifted her into the buggy. She envisioned Emma waving from the porch and heard the *clip-clop* of Nellie's hooves. If only she could be with them again.

Leaving the window, she reached for the blue fabric, recalling how Emma had helped her cut the pattern. Miriam settled onto the bedside chair, threaded her needle and started to sew. The rhythmic in and out of the needle and thread through the cotton cloth brought comfort and soothed her troubled spirit as she labored in the night. With each stitch she remembered the special world she had left behind.

At last, her work completed, she slipped into the Amish dress and gazed at her reflection in the mirror. Staring back at her was a new woman who was ready to leave the *Englisch* world behind. Miriam didn't need or want the things of this life. Instead she yearned for the *plain* way of the Amish. She longed to embrace their faith in God, their love of family and their appreciation for hard work and simple blessings.

Abram may have already moved on with his life, but even without him at her side—as heartbreaking as that would be—Miriam wanted his faith.

She glanced away from the mirror, no longer needing to see her reflection. She knew who she was. She was an Amish woman who was eager to return home.

TWENTY-EIGHT

Standing on the hillside, Abram looked down at his farm and Isaac's dairy in the distance. Emma and the dairyman would soon marry. Daniel would have a mother, and Abram's sister would find the happiness she deserved.

Abram was happy for her. He turned back to his work and pulled the wire more tightly around the fence post, thankful for physical labor that occupied his hands. If only it could occupy his mind, as well. No matter what he did, his thoughts were always on Miriam and how much he longed to see her again.

Once the wire was attached, Abram stared up at the sky. The sun peered out from between the clouds and the warm hint of spring filled the air.

"A young man's fancy…" He thought of the adage about a man's heart turning to love and shook his head.

He was no longer a young man and he had found his love.

The sound of a car engine caught his attention. He turned, seeing the Amish Taxi driving from town along the fork in the road.

A friend must be coming to visit Emma. Abagail Keim had stopped by twice since she and her mother had kept Daniel. Perhaps she was visiting again.

Turning back to his work, Abram ignored the sound of the car door slamming. Then, realizing he needed to be considerate of Abagail's feelings, he turned to wave a greeting.

But what he saw made his heart lurch.

He blinked, unwilling to believe his eyes.

An Amish woman wearing a blue dress stepped from the taxi. She was slender, with golden-brown hair, and stared at him from a distance. Then she waved and started running, past the house and up the hill.

"Abram," she called. "I've come home."

His heart burst with joy. He dropped his tools and raced to meet her, his arms wide as she ran into his embrace.

"Oh, Miriam," he sighed, inhaling the sweet smell of her. "I have missed you so."

"I...I had to leave, Abram. I had to try to find Hannah. But she was gone. I thought I would learn to live in the city, yet my heart broke each day there without you."

She pulled back and stared into his eyes as if she, too, couldn't believe they were together again.

"I kept hearing your voice, Abram. You kept saying, 'Come home to me.' I knew you were calling me back to Willkommen."

"Miriam, I love you. I have loved you since the first moment I saw you. We will make this work."

"Yah," she said with a twinkle in her eyes and pointing to the blue frock she wore. "Did you see the dress I made? Emma taught me how to cut the fabric, and I finished it in Atlanta. Stitching it together by hand made me realize where my heart really wanted to be. With you, Abram, living the Amish life and being a member of the Amish church."

"Oh, Miriam. You are all I have ever wanted."

He lowered his lips to hers and then, scooping her into

his arms, he twirled her around and around. They kissed until they were dizzy and giddy with laugher.

Their playfulness turned serious as he drew her even closer and looked deeply into her eyes. "I love you, Miriam Miller, and I always will. You bring joy to my heart and to my home. Plus you were right about voicing my contrition aloud. I talked to the bishop about my past. That weight has been removed from my heart, which is now filled to overflowing with my love for you."

Again, they kissed. She molded into his embrace, their hearts entwined, as Abram wrapped her tightly in his arms, never wanting to let her go.

EPILOGUE

"I packed cheese and bread and fruit for the journey." Emma handed the basket to Miriam, who placed it on the floor of the buggy.

Miriam smiled with gratitude. "You have done too much."

Emma waved off the comment. "Promise you will write to us when you arrive in Ethridge and let us know about the wedding plans? Isaac and Daniel and I want to be there to celebrate with you and Abram."

"I'll write and let you know, even before the date is published at church."

"It is *gut* that Abram and our *datt* have reconciled. That is your doing, Miriam."

She shook her head. "No, Emma, the credit goes to Abram. He had to forgive himself. Once he did, he was able to ask forgiveness from his father. Their relationship, at least through the mail, seems strong, although I have to admit that I'm worried about meeting him."

"Our *datt* has a gruff exterior but a heart of gold."

Miriam rolled her eyes and laughed. "Now I'm even more concerned."

"I promise, our parents will love you."

"You're sure?" Miriam asked.

"*Yah*. As Daniel says, 'Cross my heart.'"

Both women laughed for a long moment and then the smile on Emma's face waned. "I am glad you will stay in Ethridge until the investigation is over and all those involved in the trafficking ring are brought to justice. Isaac saw more reporters in town, asking questions. He fears the stories they write in their newspapers will draw attention to Willkommen."

"Abram says I will be safer in Tennessee. We wouldn't be able to go if you and Isaac hadn't offered to take care of the farm."

"It is good we live close." Isaac approached the buggy. "Abagail's twin brothers will help, as well."

Daniel left the workshop and skipped toward them, with Abram and Bear following close behind. The boy blew into the wooden train whistle Abram had made. The deep, soulful sound filled the air.

"Daniel, you must not blow the whistle around Nellie," Emma cautioned lovingly. "You will spook her for sure."

The boy hurried to Emma's side, his eyes wide with excitement. "Abram said he will teach me woodworking when he and Miriam return."

Emma touched his cheek lovingly. "That is something to look forward to, *yah*."

The boy nodded then turned to Miriam and smiled slyly as if he had a secret to share. "*Mamm* baked cookies for your basket."

"Your new *mamm* is very thoughtful." Miriam loved the way Daniel had accepted Emma into his life.

"How many of the cookies did you eat, Daniel?" Abram asked as he neared.

"More than *Datt* thought I should."

The adults laughed and watched as Daniel chased Bear around the yard.

Abram's face grew serious. He turned to Isaac. "Be

careful, my friend. There is talk that this hijacking opera-
tion is large. More could happen. Ned told me."

"I have heard the same. I will take care of Emma and
be on guard lest anything else occurs. And do not worry.
We will not divulge where you and Miriam have gone.
Your secret will be safe with us."

"But we will eagerly await your return." Emma
squeezed Miriam's hand. "The talk at the market is that
Samuel will have a long recovery, although Ned Quigley
is doing a good job as acting sheriff."

"If he can do enough," Abram mused. "At least he is
searching for Sarah."

"The Petersville police chief is helping him," Isaac
added. "It appears he was not involved in the corruption."

"Ned promised to write me if he learns anything new,"
Miriam said as she hugged her soon-to-be sister-in-law and
then Isaac. "Abram and I continue to pray."

"*Gott* will answer us with good news, I am sure," Abram
said before he hugged his sister and helped Miriam into the
buggy. "We must go, if we are to catch the bus to Ethridge."

Isaac shook Abram's hand and then slapped his back.
"The twins will drive your buggy back this afternoon when
they come to work on the farm."

"They will be good farmers by the time we return."

Abram climbed in beside Miriam and lifted the reins.

Daniel ran to stand between Isaac and Emma and raised
his hand in farewell as the buggy turned onto the roadway,
heading to Willkommen.

"Take care of Bear and Gus," Abram said as he glanced
back over his shoulder. Ezra Jacobs's beagle ambled out of
the barn, wagging his tail. The well-being of the old dog
had tugged at Abram's heart until he had found Gus wandering aimlessly in the woods.

Daniel waved. "*Yah*, we will."

When the farm and Isaac's sweet family were out of sight, Miriam shrugged out of her cape, enjoying the warmth of the day.

"The flowers will be in bloom soon," she said, eyeing the countryside as they passed by.

"The letter from my mother said she is painting the house and watching her celery grow," Abram shared.

Miriam laughed, remembering the celery served at Isaac and Emma's wedding. "There are many customs I must get used to, Abram."

"I will help you learn them all."

"What if your parents don't like the woman you have chosen to marry?"

"Ah, but they will love you. After the wedding, we will move into the house next door that belonged to my *grossdaadi*, my grandfather, and my *mammi*, my grandmother. It will be a time to reconcile with the family I left behind." He gently elbowed her, his eyes twinkling. "And a time to get to know my new wife."

"A honeymoon," she said, smiling. "As the *Englisch* say."

He laughed and took her hand. "Hopefully, *Gott* will bless us soon with children. Lots of children who will help their mother in the kitchen and their father in the fields."

"And in the workshop," she added. "Your business is growing, Abram. So many people at the market love your work. I knew they would."

"You encouraged me, Miriam. For that I am thankful."

He pulled back on the reins and the buggy came to a stop. Turning to face her, he tucked a strand of hair behind her ear. "Most of all, I am thankful for you, Miriam. That you came into my life and set me free from the past."

He kissed her for a very long time. Her heart leaped

for joy and was filled with hope for the future. A future with Abram.

She raised her face to the sun, peering through the clouds. Spring, a wedding, children in the future and her Amish protector who had saved her life and saved her heart.

As Nellie started moving again, Abram wrapped his arm around Miriam's waist and pulled her close. "Soon we will be one, Miriam. An Amish man and an *Englisch* woman—"

"An *Englischer* turned Amish," she added with a smile.

"What could be better?" he asked.

"Nothing," she sighed.

Nothing could be better than living the rest of her life with Abram at her side.

"Thank You, God," she whispered. "Thank you, Abram."

He raised his brow and leaned closer. "Did you say something?"

"I said thank you for saving me, for loving me and for asking me to be your wife."

"Our life will be *gut*," he said with a flick of the reins.

"Yah." Miriam smiled. "Our life will be very, very *gut*."

* * * * *

If you enjoyed AMISH REFUGE, look for these other titles by Debby Giusti.

THE AGENT'S SECRET PAST
PLAIN TRUTH
PLAIN DANGER

Dear Reader,

I hope you enjoyed *Amish Refuge*, the first book in my AMISH PROTECTORS series. Amish widower Abram Zook never expected a battered woman to appear on his front porch in the middle of the night. Especially not an *Englisch* woman. But Miriam Miller's car has been hijacked, her mother's been murdered and her younger sister carted off to who knows where. Miriam needs to hole up and stay safe, and what better place than on an Amish farm.

This story is about forgiveness. If you struggle to let go of a painful past, I hope Abram and Miriam's journey will touch your heart and bring you to a place of new beginnings. I'm praying for you!

I love to hear from readers. Email me at debby@debbygiusti.com or write me c/o Love Inspired, 195 Broadway, 24th Floor, New York, NY 10007. Visit me at www.DebbyGiusti.com and at www.facebook.com/debby.giusti.9.

As always, I thank God for bringing us together through this story.

Wishing you abundant blessings,
Debby

*An FBI agent must protect his prime suspect in a series
of bombings...without falling for her.*

*Read on for an excerpt from Valerie Hansen's
SPECIAL AGENT,
the next book in the exciting new series,
CLASSIFIED K-9 UNIT.*

Katerina Garwood was halfway between one of the stables
and the house, heading for her old suite, when she saw an
imposing black vehicle pass beneath the ornate wrought
iron arch at the foot of the drive. Unexpected company was
all she needed. If her father came outside to see who it was
and caught her trespassing on his precious property he'd be
furious. Well, so be it. There was no way she could run and
hide in time to avoid encountering the new arrival—and
perhaps her irate dad, as well.

Chin high, she paused in the wide, hard-packed drive
and shaded her eyes. The SUV reminded her of one that
had assisted the county sheriff on the worst day of her
life. The day when all her dreams of a happy future had
vanished like a puff of smoke.

Dark-tinted windows kept her from getting a good look
at the driver until he stopped, opened his door and stepped
partway out. Prepared to tell him to go to the house if he
needed to speak to someone in charge, she took one look
and was momentarily speechless. The blond, blue-eyed

man was so imposing and had such a powerful presence he sent her usually normal reactions whirling. When he spoke, his deep voice magnified those unsettling feelings.

"Katerina Garwood?"

"Do I know you?"

"No, but I know you. I'm Special Agent West. I'd like to talk to you about Vern Kowalski."

"I have nothing to say." She started to turn away.

"This is not a social call, Ms. Garwood." He flashed a badge and blocked her path. "I suggest you reconsider."

"FBI? You have to be kidding. I am so normal, so boring, that until recently people hardly noticed me."

"They do now, I take it."

She blushed and rolled her eyes. "Oh, yeah."

"Then you'll understand why I need to speak with you."

Don't miss
SPECIAL AGENT by Valerie Hansen,
available wherever
Love Inspired® Suspense ebooks are sold.

www.LoveInspired.com

LISEXP0517